Valley of Hate

VALLEY OF HATE

Gene Tuttle

AVALON BOOKS
THOMAS BOUREGY AND COMPANY, INC.
NEW YORK

PRINTED IN THE UNITED STATES OF AMERICA
BY HADDON CRAFTSMEN, SCRANTON, PENNSYLVANIA

Valley of Hate

CHAPTER ONE

It was almost dusk when Silent Slade and Irish O'Day rode slowly across the railroad tracks and got their first real look at Tecoma. They shaded their eyes against the Arizona sunset and gazed at the little depot. Then they glanced at the building—atop a big hill—that housed both a saloon and a restaurant. Those were the only signs of human habitation.

"That's Tecoma?" Irish asked as he shifted in his saddle and looked sideways at his tall, wiry partner. "That's the whole town?"

"Yep, that's it," said Silent, "unless they're using some kind of a camouflage to hide the other buildings, but I doubt it."

"I hope I can get something to eat," Irish sighed.

The two men rode up the deeply rutted wagon road that led to the restaurant and tied up their horses at the long hitchrack.

1

As they were eating, a man from the saloon opened the door between the two establishments and squinted at the two strangers. Then he went back, and Irish could see him sit down at a poker table with two other men.

After supper, Silent and Irish sauntered into the saloon and looked around. The three men were playing poker, and the one who had come to open the door looked up at them and grinned. He was short and fat, with a moonlike face that was half-hidden because of the green eyeshade that he wore.

"What'll you gents have?" he asked.

"Just looking around," replied Silent as they moved over to the table and looked at the game.

"Care to join us?" said the man. "Not much to do around here."

Silent squinted at Irish, who grinned and nodded, so they sat down and were dealt into the game.

Silent watched closely as the man with the eyeshade dealt the first hand. Then the man next to him shuffled the cards clumsily, but managed to deal them out. Silent smiled to himself as the man who had dealt the hand won. Next it was Irish's turn, and everything went fine.

Then the deal came to Silent, who felt of the cards and grinned as he shuffled them. Then he paused and looked at the men around the table.

"Just to get things straight, gents, I feel in this penny-ante game we should keep it on the square," he said in a low but piercing voice.

The men glanced quickly at one another. Then the man with the eyeshade, who was the saloon proprietor, squinted at Silent.

"Meaning what, stranger?" he asked.

"Let me show you something," said Silent,

stacking the deck in front of him. "I'll deal, but I don't want anyone to pick up his cards till I tell you to."

"Sounds crazy to me," grunted one of the men.

"Let him show you," urged Irish.

The men agreed. Silent shuffled the deck again, then quickly, with one hand, dealt five cards to each man. Then he put the deck down.

"Turn your cards over, face up, on the table. This doesn't count."

The men glanced at the proprietor, who nodded. Slowly he turned his cards over; they were all low cards. The next man turned his and also had low cards. The third man had one face card and four low cards. Then Irish turned his cards over. He had four kings and a jack. The men gasped. Silent then reached out and turned his own cards over: three queens, an ace, and a jack!

"How in blazes didja do that?" gasped the proprietor.

"I believe you get the point, gents," said Silent as he leaned forward and racked in all the cards, piling them into the deck and shuffling them several times, then having the proprietor cut the deck.

"We'll keep the game on the level," said Silent as he dealt the cards. "That's been my business for many years, but I never use it unless I have to in a poker game."

They all nodded. After going around the table a second time, Silent decided that they had better check out.

"I wish there was a hotel here," he said, pushing back his chair. "Ain't even a stable where you can feed a horse."

"And that's a fact," agreed the proprietor.

"Tecoma ain't no town, tall fellow. If I had a bed, I'd offer it to you and your pardner; but all I've got is a cot to sleep on."

"It's about twenty miles to Moolock," offered one of the men. "The road ain't too good, but you can get a bed in Moolock."

Silent yawned and squinted at Irish O'Day, who was a few years younger, broad of shoulder, and somewhat stocky. Irish was slightly under six feet—when his red hair was brushed down. His face was tanned from the sun and his cobalt blue eyes seemed amused at everything, but they turned a hard blue when trouble appeared. His mouth was a mere slash in his face until he broke into a grin, and then everyone liked Irish.

"What do you think about it, Irish?" asked Silent. "Shall we gird up our broncs and hie away for this Moolock town?"

"Just so well as not, I reckon," said Irish. "Might as well be riding as sitting here."

"You men came in from Bearpaw?" asked the saloon proprietor.

"Yeah," nodded Silent. "We came in over the Grayling trail. Some darned fool told us that there was a lot of available land up there—land that was pretty rich; but he lied, as usual. What kind of country is this Moolock?"

"Cows, mostly. Lot of good outfits. Frank Allenby owns the Half-Circle Cross, the biggest outfit."

Silent looked curiously at Irish, who regarded him innocently. The thin cowboy was well over six feet, even without his high heels and tall Stetson. His face was long, heavily lined, and bronzed the color of an Indian. His cheekbones were prominent and he had a long nose that was slightly irregular. Silent was not handsome. Some remarked at times that he had the face of the devil—that is, until he smiled, and then everyone joined in smiling.

Silent and Irish cashed in what chips they had, bought some tobacco from the proprietor, and went out to the hitchrack.

As they started to untie their horses, Irish grunted wonderingly. He had ridden a roan horse into Tecoma, but the horse he was looking at now was decidedly gray. Its head was hanging low with fatigue.

He called softly to Silent, who was doing a little swearing over his own discovery.

"I've got me a pinto," grunted Silent as Irish blurted out the fact that he had drawn a tired gray.

There were only the two horses at the hitchrack. Irish scratched a match and discovered that whoever had made the substitution had changed saddles, too.

"We've still got our saddles," he declared. "Now what in blazes do you know about that?"

Silent untied his pinto and led it into the light from the saloon door, where he appraised the animal slowly. It was sore-footed and weary. Irish walked over beside him, leading the gray, and was about to call to those inside the saloon to come out and help them wonder over it all, when a voice yelled out from the darkness:

"Put up your hands, doggone you!"

A revolver flashed and the bullet bit a splinter out of the sidewalk. With an almost automatic movement, Silent drew and fired at the flash; and at the same moment he darted out of the light and flung himself flat on the ground. Irish went headlong out of the illumination, rolled down the hill, and came to rest behind a big rock.

"Gosh dang you, what did you do that for, Forty?" wailed the same voice from the darkness. "Who in tarnation told you to shoot, anyway?"

"Don't walk into that light, Swan River!" cautioned another voice, presumably belonging to Forty. "They didn't go far. I've got to fix that damn gun of mine. It's too easy on the pull. Don't get in that light, you darned fool!"

The three men in the saloon had moved to the doorway, wondering aloud what it was all about. The proprietor carried a sawed-off shotgun, and at the sight of him, the one called Swan River spoke quickly:

"Hey, Pierson! This is the sheriff!"

"Hello, Swan River," called the saloon proprietor. "What's all the ruckus about, anyway?"

"Don't get in that light!" warned the deputy, Forty Dollar Dion, whose gun was easy on the trigger. "I tell you, they didn't get far away."

"Who are you looking for?" asked Pierson.

"The men who owned them two horses," replied Swan River Smith, the sheriff of Moolock County. "They stuck up a train this afternoon, and we've been on their trail ever since. That's their gray and pinto."

"Hey, Sheriff!" called Silent.

"Listening."

"Then listen closely. Those aren't our horses. I reckon the three men in the doorway can tell you that we rode a roan and a bay into this place late this afternoon, and that we've been here ever since. We just found out that somebody traded horses with us, and we were admiring them in the light."

"That's the truth," said Pierson, the proprietor.

"They sure did ride a roan and a bay in here, Sheriff."

"Well." The sheriff seemed a bit dubious. "If you say so, Pierson, I'll take your word for it. C'mon, gents."

Silent and Irish sauntered back into the light and looked at Swan River Smith and his elongated deputy. The sheriff was a small gray-haired man with a pair of eyes as hard as granite. Forty Dollar Dion was almost as tall as Silent and sad of face. He walked with a loose-jointed shamble that would cause one to suspect that he might fall apart at any time.

"I'm the sheriff of this here county," said Swan River after a close scrutiny of the two cowpunchers. "Name's Smith."

Silent introduced himself and Irish, and the sheriff suggested that they all adjourn to the bar to wet their thirst. As they turned to go up the three steps from the street, Silent stumbled, falling against the sheriff, and they almost went down, but Forty Dollar grabbed the sheriff and helped hold him up while Silent went to his knees.

"Damn clumsy of me," grunted Silent. "Are you all right, Sheriff?"

Swan River spat to one side and took a deep breath as he felt himself all over. Then he replied:

"Yeah, I'm all right. What happened?"

"Loose board in the steps," grunted Silent as he got to his feet and dusted his knees off.

They walked into the saloon and went up to the bar where Pierson was ready to serve them. The four men lined up at the bar: Silent, Swan River, Forty Dollar, and Irish. They all placed their orders.

"You danged near—" Forty Dollar, glass in

hand, squinted past the sheriff at Silent, who was sipping at his glass. The deputy swallowed hard and moved around Swan River and came in closer to Silent, squinting at the front of Silent's shirt. On the left side of his shirt was a five-pointed star.

"Are—are you a sheriff?" queried Forty.

Silent shook his head. "Nope—why?"

"Whatcha doing wearing a sheriff's star, then?"

Swan River glanced at the star. Then quickly his right hand went to his flimsy vest where it discovered there was no badge. He leaned forward past Forty and squinted at the star, then up at Silent's face.

"My badge!" he snorted.

Silent laughed. "Reckon it wanted a change of scenery." He took off the badge and handed it back to Swan River.

"How in blazes did that ever happen?" grunted Forty.

"It was easy for Silent," laughed Irish. "When Silent fell out there, he took the badge off the sheriff's vest."

"That easy, huh?" grunted Swan River as he fastened the badge back on his vest. "I'll be damned! I'll buy a drink to that."

Forty shook his head in disbelief as he looked at Silent.

"You danged near killed me," the deputy declared mournfully. "My gun went off accidental. I had sense enough to sidestep; and your bullet poked a hole in the air just after I left. And it ain't like me to think fast, either."

"Well," grinned Silent, "you can't blame me, pardner. One of you yelled for us to put up our hands and the other one shot at us."

"Excuse him, if you can," said the sheriff. "I

can't. Here's happy days and a blanket at night."
He looked at Forty. "Did you take a good look at
them horses, Forty?"

"Uh-huh," nodded the deputy. "I was right,
Swan."

"The question is, where did they go from here?"
said Swan River.

"I'll betcha forty dollars they headed for Bearpaw," said Forty. "They've got fresh horses."

"And good horses," added Irish mournfully.

"I never heard of a lost horse that wasn't a
good one," grinned the sheriff. "Nobody ever lost
a bad one. Ha, ha, ha! Well, there ain't no use
trying to follow them two fellows. Our horses are
plumb whipped; so we might as well go home, I
reckon."

"How much did they get?" asked Silent.

"I don't know—yet. They blew the safe on the
express car and took what was in it. Cut the train
in two and made their getaway near where they
had their horses staked out.

"But the engineer got a look at the horses and,
as soon as they pulled into Moolock, he told me
about it. Me and Forty cut straight across the hills
and were lucky enough to spot them.

"Since then we've sure burnt up horseflesh.
Comes night and we kinda lose track of them; so
we heads for here and finds that pinto and gray,
standing plumb in the light. You can't blame us
for the mistake, can you?"

Silent laughed and shook his head. It was all
clear to him now, and he did not blame the sheriff
and deputy.

"I reckon we'll go back to Moolock with you,"
he said. "Maybe them two horses are as fresh as
yours, Sheriff."

"Yeah, sure, let's go," nodded Swan River. "It's a long ride back there."

"There's no place for us to stay here," said Irish.

"Do you boys know anyone down in Moolock, Slade?" asked Swan River. Then he mentioned some of the people who lived around there.

"Nope, don't really know the folks there. Me and Irish rode into Bearpaw from over the Grayling trail. We kinda had an idea we'd like to do some gold mining, and we was told that there was plenty of good ground left up there; but there wasn't an inch. By golly, a bird has to keep in the trees to keep from being a trespasser."

"Well, let's pull out," said Forty. "I'm achin' to get to my own bed."

"That's nothing new," grunted Swan River as they filed out of the saloon.

They told Tecoma good-bye, mounted the jaded horses, and headed for Moolock, Swan River and Silent in the lead, with Irish and Forty Dollar bringing up the rear.

"Seems to me maybe I've heard of Moolock before," observed Silent as they jogged along over the dim road through the pines. "The name is a bit familiar. You spoke of a fellow named Allenby. Now it comes back to me."

"Frank Allenby," said the sheriff. "He's the biggest man in Moolock County."

"To hear him tell it," said Forty Dollar, "his family is in charge of the rising and setting of the sun. It's a fact. He tells it when to come up and when to go down."

"Didn't Allenby send some young fellow to the pen a while ago?"

"Yeah. A young fellow by the name of Bud Bell. Allenby didn't exactly send him to the peniten-

tiary; but he was responsible for it. Bud's out now.
I ain't seen him yet. Maybe he hates me for what
I done, but I had to do it. The Bell family are kind
of strong on hate."

"Hate!" snorted Forty Dollar disgustedly.
"Everybody around here hates someone. Allenby
is probably the worst when it comes to hate. Why,
he even hates God at times—if a person can go
that far."

"You're prejudiced," grunted Swan River.

"I am, am I? Don't Allenby hate us? He hates
Jack Merton because he's successful as a cattleman. He hates Joe Bass because nothing seems to
bother him. I heard him cuss out Ed Clayton because he said Clayton wasn't giving him a square
deal on the sale of his horses and cows. And you
say there's no hate?"

"All right," grunted Swan River as he turned
to Silent. "Getting back to Allenby, he bought the
Half-Circle Cross from Ronald Winter about three
years ago. Allenby is from Philadelphia. Never
seen a cow ranch until he hit this country. Hank
Bell nested on what Winter claimed as his own
ranch, but Winter didn't own it.

"There was bad blood between Winter and old
Hank. Winter tried in every way to oust old Hank.
Hank's cows turned up missing; some of them had
their throats cut. But old Hank stuck. One day
him and Winter met on the street in Moolock and
shot it out. Winter got a bullet through one lung
and old Hank got his right arm crippled for life.

"It kinda put a crimp into old Hank as a gunman; so he spent all his time giving his son Bud
a six-gun education. And Bud was a danged good
pupil. Then Winter sold out to Allenby, who tried
to oust Bell, but the old boy had a title to his ranch.

It's a mighty sore spot with Allenby because Hank's place has the best spring in the range."

"Did they stop killing Hank's cattle?" asked Silent.

Swan River Smith chuckled. "Yeah, you might say they did. The Bible says something about an eye for an eye and a tooth for a tooth. Anyway, Allenby got the deadwood on Bud Bell and sent him up for five years; but the law let him out in two years and a few days. Now I reckon Allenby is shaking in his boots for fear Bud will make him pay for that two years."

"Allenby is rich, isn't he?" Slade asked.

"Yeah, I suppose he's pretty well fixed," replied the sheriff.

"And I'll tell you why," added Forty Dollar. "Allenby is so stingy that he wouldn't pay two bits for a front seat at the Custer battle if the original actors would come back and play it. It's an honest fact. To my way of thinking, Allenby is a big jughead, with too much money and a soul so danged thin that it squeaks in the wind like a fiddle string. He wants everybody to know he's from Philly-del-fee."

"That ain't nothing agin him," said the sheriff.

"Not that part," agreed Forty Dollar. "I admire him for getting out of that place. I've been there—"

"Whoa, Forty Dollar Dion!" snorted Swan River. "You mean you've heard about it."

"I've heard that men don't value their lives very highly in Moolock," said Silent, changing the subject somewhat.

"That so, eh?" The sheriff seemed surprised.

"Some as cheap as five thousand dollars."

"Cheap?" blurted Forty Dollar. "Why, I could point out a lot that wouldn't be worth that much per bale. Five thousand! Say, if I was Saint Peter I wouldn't even accept souls from Moolock, unless they came prepaid."

"Forty Dollar is a pessimist," explained the sheriff quickly.

"I am like blazes!" snorted Forty Dollar. "I'm a good judge of character. That's what I am! Just telling it the way it is."

"I think we'll like Moolock," said Irish.

"Well, some does," said the deputy. "I know at least a hundred that couldn't even think of leaving there."

"Love their little town, eh?" Irish said.

"No—they're stuck in the little cemetery," chuckled Forty Dollar. "Ha, ha, ha, ha! I'll drink with you in Moolock."

They all laughed as they rode down the last of the steep grades into Moolock Valley. The moon had lifted, bathing the hills and valley in a faint glow. Far off to the left a light twinkled from a window.

"That's the 27A ranch," said the sheriff. "Joe Bass owns it. Joe's part Nez Perce. Minds his own business. Been here a long time. Ships quite a lot of stock."

"Moolock is the shipping center, isn't it?" asked Silent.

"Most of it goes from here. It's kind of in the center of the valley; so mostly everybody trades there." The sheriff paused, eased his body in the saddle, and looked at Silent. "I was just wondering what you meant about human life being cheap in Moolock."

"Nothing much," laughed Silent. "I heard that a man—a certain man—only put that much value on his life."

"Well, I don't know," grunted the sheriff thoughtfully. "I suppose that some folks feel that way about money. I'd hate to sell my life for any amount."

"And yet you take a chance every day for so much less."

"Yeah, that's a fact. You fellows aim to get jobs over here?"

"Perhaps. A fellow's got to eat."

"They sure do. You might see Allenby. Jack Merton might need a man. He runs the Arrowhead brand and his iron is on a lot of cows. Them two are the biggest outfits. You'd like Jack. He's young and full of ambition."

"Do you think we'd like Allenby?" Silent asked.

"Hmm, well, you might. It takes all kinds of folks to make up a world. What's meat for one man is poison for another."

"We'll nose around," said Silent.

"Might as well," said Swan River. "Say, Slade, why didja trip us up and steal my badge in Tecoma?"

"Just testing my skill," chuckled Silent. "You see, I used to be a magician, and I worked with people on the stage, taking things from them without their knowing it. I just wanted to see how good my touch still was."

"Magician, eh?" grunted the sheriff. "We had one come through here a few years back with a road show. Man, was he clever. Pulled rabbits out of a silk hat."

"I don't know how he ever did that," grunted

Forty Dollar. "I tried it, but I never got anything."

"It takes a lot of practice," said Irish. "Silent's always pulling something."

"I don't know how you could stand it," grunted Forty Dollar.

"I got used to it," laughed Irish. "Maybe he'll show you a few things while we're visiting here."

It was about one o'clock in the morning when they rode into the town of Moolock, stabled their horses, and got a room at the one little hotel. They were too tired to investigate the town, and even the hard mattress of their bed felt like down feathers.

"It's funny how things work out," observed Silent as they stretched out in bed. "We never had any idea of running into this place."

"It's the same Allenby, ain't it?" asked Irish.

"Sure. Bob Freeman said in his letter that it was Allenby of Moolock; so it must be the same person. He spoke about the fellow that Allenby sent to the penitentiary, and about the old man."

"They are the ones that are stealing Allenby's cows, eh?" Irish asked.

"The ones Allenby said he'd pay us five thousand for, if we could get them convicted. But he said it had to be them." Silent sighed. "Allenby wants his detective work done on commission, Irish. And it's got to prove what he wants—or forget it. He's afraid of his life, that's what's the matter with him. And he values it at five thousand dollars."

"Probably all it's worth," laughed Irish.

Silent Slade had often tried to sniff out cattle rustlers. But he did not accept an assignment where he was told who was guilty—before he had a chance to learn the truth for himself. He was too good a detective for that.

Silent's ability had led him to working at times for Wells Fargo, the Pinkerton Agency, and various ranchers' groups. It was while he was on one of these assignments that he met Irish O'Day, who had a desire to see the country. They teamed up and worked together on many cases.

Before that, at a tender age, Silent Slade had left his home and joined a circus in the East. An old-timer took a liking to the young lad and began to teach him all he knew about magic and such. Silent became tops in the field, learning how to throw his voice, how to hypnotize people, and other things. He had appeared all over the world, but he tired of that life and decided he wanted to go West and become a cowboy.

Sometimes he wondered if that had been a mistake.

CHAPTER TWO

Early the following morning Chet Hobson, foreman of the Half-Circle Cross, and Omaha Olsen,
one of the Half-Circle Cross cowboys, rode through
the main street of Moolock to the edge of town.
Then they cut across a flat and headed toward the
big loading corrals near the railroad depot. A string
of cattle cars were being shunted onto a spur track
by a freight engine as they rode up to the corral
fence and tied up their horses.

Chet Hobson was a thin-faced, raw-boned man
whose hair was dusted with gray and whose
humped shoulders and bowed legs gave him the
appearance of someone carrying a mighty burden.
Omaha Olsen was taller than Hobson and many
years younger.

The engine uncoupled and went puffing back
toward the depot, while Hobson and Olsen crossed
the track, circled the corrals and stopped. For a

space of several seconds, they surveyed the empty corrals, and then as if by mutual consent, they climbed to the wide plank at the top and gazed across the different pens, their faces filled with an expression of wonderment.

Then Hobson circled to the main gate, where he sat down and looked at the broken padlock, which dangled from a twisted staple. Omaha Olsen came up and peered down at it. Then he took out his tobacco and papers and calmly began rolling a cigarette, while Hobson turned and gazed off into the rolling hills.

"They done busted the lock," said Omaha.

Hobson turned and squinted at him, but did not reply. The broken lock needed no further comment.

"Three hundred of them critters, too," said Omaha. "And Allenby will just about bust a gizzard. I can see him commencing to get red and swell up like a carbuncle. This'll sure ache him all over."

"You'd ache if somebody stole that many two-year-old Herefords from you," retorted Hobson.

"Hell, I'd ache if I ever had that many. Now, what in blazes will we do with these cattle cars?"

Hobson got slowly to his feet and brushed off his overalls. He hitched up his belt and shook his head. "Let Clayton worry about that," he said. "C'mon."

They walked back to their horses, mounted, and rode back into town. The sheriff was still asleep, but Hobson hammered on his office door and woke him up.

"What's the matter?" grumbled Swan River, looking at Hobson through half-closed eyes.

"Last night we had three hundred two-year-old

Herefords in the loading corrals, Sheriff," replied Hobson. "They were to be loaded this morning, but somebody smashed the padlock on the main gate and swiped the whole herd. Corrals are empty."

Swan River scratched his head thoughtfully.

"Well," he said slowly, "that was worth taking. Smashed the padlock, eh? That's a penitentiary offense. Took three hundred Half-Circle Cross Herefords, eh? Gosh! Somebody held up the train yesterday, too, Chet. Danged country is going to the dogs! Allenby know?"

"Not yet. We just found it out."

"We better find Clayton," suggested Omaha. "He'll likely want to see about them cars."

"I'll get some clothes on right away and see what I can find," offered the sheriff, turning back into the office.

Hobson and Omaha walked up to the hotel where they found Ed Clayton, the cattle-buyer, just ready to leave for the loading corrals. Clayton was a big man, about thirty-five, without an ounce of fat on his huge frame. He dressed well and was an inveterate gambler, a plunger. His eyes were still heavy from a long session of poker at the Elk Saloon.

In a few words Hobson told the cattle-buyer what had happened.

"Sounds like a blasted fairy story," snorted Clayton. "You know what I mean, Hobson; it don't seem possible."

Hobson nodded shortly. He and Clayton had never been very fond of each other.

"Maybe it doesn't sound possible," Hobson said slowly. "But they're gone—the padlock's been smashed. What about your cattle cars?"

"And nothing to put them in," muttered Clayton. "Well, I'll have to see what can be done. Want to walk up to the depot with me?"

"All right," nodded Hobson. "Allenby will be here pretty soon."

The freight engine was still at the depot when the three men walked onto the platform. The depot agent was talking with the engineer, and he turned and looked at the approaching men.

"Someone stole our cattle," said Clayton.

"The engineer was just telling me that there was no stock on the loading corrals," said the agent. "What happened?"

"Someone last night smashed the padlock and stole all three hundred cows," sighed Hobson.

"What are you going to do?" asked the agent, looking at Clayton.

"I have no use now for the cars," replied Clayton. "I'm certainly sorry about it."

"Yeah," nodded the agent. "Well, you can't be blamed. Who in blazes would ride into town and remove three hundred head, and no one see or hear them?"

"That's a good question," snorted Hobson. "Moving that many cows should have made some noise—and the smashing of the padlock." He turned and looked back toward the corrals, which were possibly eight hundred feet away from the depot. "It should have made noise enough to be heard up here."

"I didn't hear a thing," grunted the agent. "I was asleep."

"Everyone was asleep," said Clayton. "I sure hate it about the cars."

"I'll tell you what we can do," suggested the agent. "We can send them up to Bluejoint. Old Joe

Bass has been yelling for days for cars. An' Jack Merton was here yesterday asking for some cars. They both have some cows to ship—unless someone stole them, too. Shall I take a chance?"

"Go ahead," urged Clayton. "I don't want the things. If either of them can use the cars, they're sure welcome to them."

Bluejoint was merely a siding with a loading corral about ten miles from Moolock. It was sometimes used by the ranchers of that side of the valley in making small shipments and was located about two miles from the 27A ranch owned by Joe Bass.

"I'll send word out to both Merton and Bass that they can have these cars," said the agent as he took off fast toward town.

Clayton looked down toward the empty corrals and shook his head, and the three men started back toward town. There they sat down on the hotel porch and watched for Allenby to arrive.

"What do you think he'll say?" asked Clayton.

"He'll probably explode," grinned Omaha.

"I'm not sure," said Hobson. "It may take him a while to understand just what happened. You know, Allenby doesn't think anything can go wrong for him."

"Yeah," drawled Omaha. "Like his precious son. Someday he'll learn that Harry is a no-good human, not worth the powder it would take to blow him off this earth."

"Harry's not that bad," said Clayton. "He just gets off on the wrong foot now and then. I don't think his father takes the time he should with a son."

"Too darn busy thinking about himself," grunted Omaha.

"It's tough on Mrs. Allenby and June," said Hobson. "I've seen the expression on their faces when Harry comes home drunk. Sometimes I'd like to slap him down. His tongue is sharp."

"You don't have to stay at the Half-Circle Cross," said Clayton."

"I know," said Hobson. "It's been a good home for many years, but it's not the same since Winter sold out. I've toyed with the idea of pulling out."

"Me, too," Omaha said. "You can take just so much for forty a month."

"Where would you go?" asked Clayton.

"Probably north toward Idaho and Montana," replied Hobson. "I've heard a lot about that country, but I've never been there."

"Anything would be better than working for Allenby," grunted Omaha. "I've saved up a good nest egg so I don't have to worry for a while."

"Me, too," laughed Hobson as he leaned forward in his chair, looking toward the end of the main street. "There comes the boss."

Moving toward the hotel was a buckboard drawn by a pair of cream-colored horses, and handling the reins was Frank Allenby. He was about fifty years of age, portly, and one could tell he was arrogant from the way he sat upright on the seat, as if he owned the earth and had a good mortgage on the moon and stars.

When Forty Dollar Dion had declared the night before that Allenby thought the sun rose and set because of the Allenby family, he was not so far wrong. Allenby had a square, protruding jaw, which accentuated the flatness of his cheekbones, and beneath a slightly hooked nose he wore an aggressive, brushlike gray mustache.

His suit was of black broadcloth, his boots of

the finest leather, and his hats were made to order.

Chet Hobson got up from his chair and moved out to the hitchrack. Omaha and Clayton moved out on the walk, looking at the rancher as he pulled up on his reins. Hobson tied the team, while Allenby got ponderously from the buckboard, the springs of which seemed to sigh with relief. He looked questioningly at Hobson, as though wondering why he was not at the loading corrals. He half turned and squinted at Clayton and Omaha.

"Well?" he snapped. "What in hell's going on?"

Hobson quickly explained to Allenby what had happened. As the rancher took in the information regarding his loss, he stiffened, as though to withstand a physical blow. His face paled with anger and then he hunched forward, as if to grapple with his foreman.

"Gone?" he muttered thickly. "You—you mean that someone stole all three hundred of them?"

"You might say they have," said Hobson slowly. "The padlock on the gate has been smashed. I told the sheriff about it."

"A lot of good that'll do!" snapped Allenby, shaking his head like a wounded bull. The pocketbook was Frank Allenby's vital spot, and it nauseated him to think of losing those Herefords. Then he shut his teeth with an audible snap and surged up on the boardwalk between Omaha and Clayton.

"I know all about it," said Clayton sympathetically.

"Well, I know about it, too!" roared Allenby. He was almost crying with anger. "I know who stole those Herefords. I know! I'll—"

"Go ahead and tell me who stole them," said the sheriff.

Swan River Smith had come up the walk behind the four men and had heard Allenby's statement. The big rancher whirled to face the law officer. He glared down at Swan River, but Allenby's glare did not affect Swan River in the least. The cattleman's dominating personality meant nothing to the little sheriff.

"Go ahead," urged Swan River. "I'd sure like to hear his name."

"That's my business!" snapped Allenby.

"And mine," added the sheriff. "If you know who stole your cows, tell me his name. If you don't know, Allenby, if you're only making a wild guess, keep it to yourself!"

"I'll do as I damn please!"

"Yeah?" Swan River looked him over coldly. "All right. Free speech is your right, Allenby. But if you ain't got evidence enough to back up the name you mention—the law ain't backing you."

"I don't need the blasted law! I'll be my own law!"

"Oh, yeah?" Swan River Smith shook his head as he turned and walked away, going back toward his office.

Allenby glared after him. Omaha and Clayton smiled; but Hobson's face did not change a line.

"Little pup!" sneered Allenby, half under his breath; but the sheriff was too far away to hear it.

"He isn't much," agreed Clayton.

Hobson looked sharply at the cattle-buyer. Hobson knew that Swan River Smith was a thoroughly capable officer, with a fine record behind him.

"Do you know who stole them?" asked Omaha innocently.

"Do I know who stole them?" parroted Allenby. "I do know."

"Well, let's go and get them back," suggested Omaha.

"Fool!" snorted Allenby. "Do you suppose they'd leave them where we could find them?" He spat viciously and turned to Clayton.

"When will your man be here, Ed?"

"He's due any time now," replied Clayton. "You just keep calm and let Jim Seeley work on this case. He'll put a stop to it."

"That's the detective, huh?" asked Omaha.

"Shush!" cautioned Clayton. "Don't tell everybody about it."

"I hope he can handle it," said Allenby wearily. "I can't stand losing any more stock. Freeman, the secretary of the association, promised to furnish me with a couple of men, who, he said, are the best in the world on this kind of a case. But they refused to take it. I offered them five thousand dollars for a conviction, but they refused.

"I know who is doing the dirty work, Clayton. I know just as well as if I had a confession from them; but I need evidence. Nobody else is losing stock—so they say. It's spite work, that's all it is. For over two years I've been losing cattle. I sent one man to the penitentiary, and next time I'll send two. If I don't stop them, I'll be broke. I'm going home now."

"You heard about the train robbery, didn't you?" asked Hobson.

"What robbery?" asked Allenby.

"I don't know too much, only what the sheriff told me."

"I heard late last night that the sheriff and deputy had chased the robbers to Tecoma, where they stole fresh horses and disappeared into the night," said Clayton. "Suppose they got away into the Bearpaw country."

"Suppose there's any connection between the train robbery and the rustlers?" asked Allenby.

"I doubt that," replied Clayton. "Too far apart."

Allenby nodded as he climbed into the buckboard and picked up the reins. While Hobson untied the team, the rancher looked at Clayton.

"Are you coming out to the ranch today?"

"I may be out later."

Hobson stepped back on the walk as Allenby drove the team down a way, made a U-turn, and came back, heading for the ranch. The three men watched him until he disappeared around a bend in the road.

"How about a drink?" asked Clayton.

"I sure could use one," said Omaha. "He makes me kinda dry."

"Go ahead," said Hobson. "I'll have to get back to the rest of the boys because I don't think Allenby will take the time to tell them not to ride into town."

Silent Slade and Irish O'Day had finished their breakfast at the cafe and were coming out the doorway when Frank Allenby drove past. They stopped and watched him. They looked across the street and saw the sheriff standing in the doorway of his office, also watching the departing rancher.

Silent and Irish crossed the street to the sheriff's office.

"That's the king," grunted Swan River. "You didn't bow down to him when he went past."

"I noticed you didn't, either," laughed Silent.

"Allenby ain't no woolly little sheep when he's contented," said Swan River, "so right now he's a raging wolf with nothing in sight to bite into. Somebody busted into the loading corrals last night and lifted three hundred Hereford cows that were due to take a railroad ride this morning."

"Lifted them out of the loading pens, eh?" Silent said. "I'll tell a man that's a real handy way to get them. Sheriff, I'm of the opinion that this county ain't so law-abiding that it aches."

"Naw, she ain't," agreed Forty Dollar as he came into the doorway.

"Any clues left by the light-fingered gents?" asked Irish.

Swan River shook his head. "Not a clue. There's so darn many cow tracks in this country, and no rain for two months, that you never could trail them."

"Just have to trust to luck, eh?" said Silent, showing some interest.

Irish squinted at his tall partner and grinned. He knew Silent. "Yeah—luck."

"Have much rustling to contend with?" Silent asked.

"Well, not so much. It's a queer thing about the rustling. Somebody has been stealing cows from Allenby for over two years. I've tried every scheme I could think of to nail the guilty party or parties; but they're too slick for me."

"Only from Allenby?" queried Silent.

"He's the only one that reports a loss," replied the sheriff.

"Uh-huh." Silent squinted thoughtfully. "Kinda looks like somebody has a grudge against Mr. Allenby, don't it?"

"Do you think so?" asked Forty Dollar, wishing

the new boots he was wearing didn't pinch so much.

Swan River Smith rubbed his chin thoughtfully. He knew who Allenby suspected. But the sheriff wanted to be fair. He did not know who Silent Slade and Irish O'Day were, except for their names, and he did not want to make any mistakes.

"We don't want to horn into your business," said Silent, reading the sheriff's thoughts. "It ain't nothing to us, you see. We'd kinda like to get our own horses back, though. They were real good horses."

Swan River looked up, grinning.

"I'll bet they were," he said. "I'd just like to help you get them back, to see how good they really are. C'mon, out to the stable."

They went through the back door of the sheriff's office, with Forty Dollar bringing up the rear, stamping his feet to try and stretch his new boots. If facial expressions meant anything, he was ac-complishing very little.

"These are my dude boots," he explained to Irish. "When I dress, I dress to kill."

"Yourself?" asked Irish innocently.

Forty Dollar grinned painfully and rested on his high heels, bracing one hand against the stable door, while the others went inside.

"I want you to take a look at the gray and pinto," said Swan River, pointing out the two horses in adjoining stalls. Silent looked them both over care-fully and came back beside the sheriff.

"Notice the brands?" asked the sheriff.

"Both HB animals," said Silent. "No other brands."

The sheriff squinted at the rumps of the two horses, chewing reflectively on a straw.

"I didn't need to look at the brands," he said

slowly. "I knew the two horses we were chasing yesterday. You couldn't mistake that pinto. That black head shows it up a mile away. And there ain't many grays in this here area."

"Kinda looks like Hank Bell's goose was about cooked," observed Forty Dollar, limping in from the doorway.

"That'll be about all from you," said the sheriff. "You're just pessimistic from tight boots."

"I know a way to make those boots comfortable," said Irish.

"How?" asked Forty Dollar quickly.

"Take a knife and cut them open," chuckled Irish.

"Aw, heck!" snorted Forty Dollar as they crossed the alley and went into the sheriff's office through the rear door.

Forty Dollar dropped down on a cot and managed to take off the offending footwear and put on his old boots while the others watched in amusement.

"Them that wants to be dudes can be dudes," he declared. "If I can find the drummer what sold me that pair of boots, I'll kick him seven times with each one. I want food, by golly. You fellows had breakfast yet? Yeah? Well, I reckon I can eat by my lonesome."

He grabbed his hat and left the office while the sheriff sat down at his desk. Silent sat on the corner of the desk and Irish went to the front doorway and looked out onto the street. There was an old deck of cards on the desk, and Silent picked them up and looked at them.

"They've been used plenty by Forty," grunted Swan River as he watched Silent shuffle them in one hand. Then the tall cowboy spread them out on the desk top in front of the law officer.

"Take a card, Swan River," he said.

The sheriff leaned forward and squinted at the cards. Then he took the ace of hearts and looked up at Silent.

"You take the deck, put your card back in it wherever you want, then shuffle them real good," Silent said.

The sheriff followed orders, giving the deck an extra shuffle. Then he placed it down on the desk top and squinted at Silent, who leaned forward, then looked at the deck. Then he split the deck.

"Turn over the top card in the right stack," he said.

Swan River reached out and turned over the card. It was the ace of hearts. He fingered it, then looked up at Silent, while Irish, still in the doorway, chuckled.

"Pretty good trick," grunted the sheriff.

"It's easier than stealing your badge," grinned Silent.

The sheriff put the card back in the deck and shuffled it. Then he placed the deck back on the top of the desk.

"You'll have to pull that on Forty Dollar," he said.

"He'll pull something on him," assured Irish.

The sheriff got to his feet and Silent followed him to the doorway just as a single rider came past them and dismounted at the Elk Saloon. He was a thin-faced youth and rather frail of physique.

"That's Allenby's son," said the sheriff. "Harry Allenby. The old man thinks that Harry is the finest fella that was ever whelped. I don't know

what in blazes he's ever going to make of the kid.
Allenby is so stingy that he wouldn't let the kid
go to college, yet he expects him to be President
of the United States, I reckon."

"Kind of figures to have him be a self-made
man, eh?" smiled Silent.

"Something like that," nodded Swan River. "I
like Mrs. Allenby. She's sure a nice little woman,
too nice for Allenby. And June is a dinger. June
is the daughter. She's about a year younger than
Harry, and I reckon he's about twenty-four now."

While they were discussing the Allenby family,
two more riders came toward them. Swan River
squinted thoughtfully, watching them ride to the
Elk Saloon hitchrack.

"There's Bud Bell and Sticky Clay," said the
sheriff. "Bud is the one on this side—the fellow
that Allenby sent to the penitentiary. Clay rides
for the HB outfit, and he's a gunman if there ever
was one. Oh, oh! C'mon!"

The two men tied up their horses and were going
toward the saloon door. Swan River stepped off
the boardwalk and hurried toward the saloon. After
a moment of hesitation, Silent and Irish hurried
after him.

"There's three men from Allenby's in there,"
explained Swan River as they reached the doorway. "Maybe it won't mean anything, but you never
can tell when they meet."

As they went inside, Clayton, the cattle-buyer,
was just buying some chips in a poker game, while
Omaha and Hobson were deep in the mysteries of
trying to play pool on an uneven table, on which
the cushions were as "dead" as strips of mattress.
Harry Allenby was at the bar, with a bottle at his

elbow, squinting sideways at Bud Bell and Sticky Clay, who were also at the bar, being served by Snowy Barnette, the proprietor.

As far as outward appearances went, there was no cause for the sheriff to feel any uneasiness. Bud turned his head and looked at Swan River Smith. It was their first meeting since Bud had come back from the penitentiary. But if Bud felt any malice toward the sheriff, his gray eyes did not show it at all.

"Hello, Bud," said the sheriff softly. "Going to shake hands with me?"

A slight smile flashed across the young man's thin lips and he nodded quickly, as he held out his hand.

"Why shouldn't I, Swan River?" he asked. "You wasn't to blame."

They shook hands solemnly. Omaha and Hobson stopped playing pool long enough to observe the meeting, and those in the poker game were silent until it was over. Harry Allenby took a lonesome drink and braced his elbows on the bar, hooked one heel over the bar rail, and studied the poker players.

"Howdy, Clay," said the sheriff.

Sticky Clay grinned, showing two rows of bad teeth, and motioned for the sheriff to join them in their drink.

"Invite your friends," said Sticky, noticing that Silent and Irish were with the sheriff.

"I'll take a cigar," said Silent. "Little too soon after breakfast to drink."

"That's right," grinned Clay. "I don't diagnose no man's inside workings. Is everybody set? Here's hoping you never get caught."

"Here's hoping I don't have to catch you," smiled the sheriff.

Harry Allenby laughed harshly. The saloon went silent. Swan River had spoken loud enough for everyone to hear.

"You won't have to," said Harry meaningfully. "A sheriff can do as he pleases."

Swan River's eyes narrowed, but he turned away, ignoring the implied insult. He knew that Harry had been drinking more than was good for him, and was willing to excuse him for his words. Bud was only a few feet away from Harry, with no one between them.

"You're drunk, Harry," said Ed Clayton, moving back from the poker table. "Better go out and get some fresh air."

Hobson and Omaha carefully placed their billiard cues on the pool table and moved slowly toward the bar. Harry looked at them and laughed.

"I don't need any help," he assured them, waving them back with a slight gesture of his left hand. "I can take care of myself, y'betcha. Maybe it's none of my business, but when the sheriff comes in and tries to put himself in right with a jailbird of a horse thief, I'm damned if I—" His right hand jerked toward his gun and he swayed from the bar.

Before he had finished speaking, Bud Bell had flung himself forward, and Harry Allenby went down from a smash full in the face that flattened his nose and loosened his front teeth.

He fell at the feet of Omaha and Hobson, who made no move to assist him. They were both looking at Sticky Clay, who had stepped into the center of the room, six-shooter swinging at his thigh, a grin on his lips. Harry got slowly to his feet, spitting blood, but the fight had all been taken out of him. His gun was still in its holster, and he had had enough for one day.

"You can put away your gun, Clay," said Hobson. "The kid's been drinking too much, that's all."

Sticky Clay grinned and snapped the gun back into the holster. Bud Bell's face was still white with anger, but he turned his back on the blubbering young cowboy, who was being led back to a bucket of water by Omaha Olsen.

Ed Clayton, the cattle-buyer, looked up at Swan River and said:

"Overlook that, will you, Sheriff? Harry is just a fool kid and he had too much too drink."

"I'll do the best I can," said Swan River seriously. "I hope this will be a lesson to him. Somebody'll kill him for talking too much one of these days, Clayton."

As Silent, Irish, and the sheriff walked out of the saloon, Silent remarked:

"That kid wasn't that drunk, Sheriff. How could he be? He'd only been in there about ten or fifteen minutes."

Swan River nodded. "I thought of that, but why carry it any further?"

As they headed across the street, Forty Dollar came out of the restaurant where he had heard about the ruckus.

"Just my luck!" he snorted. "Seems like I'm always eating when anything good is pulled off. If I ever want to see anything in the world, I'll have to starve, I reckon. Betcha forty dollars this won't be the end of this trouble."

"I hope you lose that forty dollars sometime," grunted the sheriff. "You've been offering that bet ever since I've knowed you."

"Nobody ever takes me up, Swan River. I'm game."

"Oh, hell, you never had that much money. I reckon I better go up to the depot and collect a lot of telegrams from the express company. They'll swamp me with them for a while, even if there wasn't a two-bit piece in that safe."

"How much did they lose?" asked Silent.

"I don't know—yet. They probably don't know yet. Anyway, there ain't a ghost of a chance to—" Swan River hesitated, cleared his throat, and headed for the depot.

"I'd say he was a square shooter," observed Silent.

"Swan River?" Forty Dollar grinned softly. "Yeah, he's all right. He'd play square with a horse thief. That's why our jail ain't hardly ever occupied. But don't ever get the idea that the little fellow ain't a fighter."

"I wouldn't choose him," smiled Silent.

They walked down the boardwalk and met Bud Bell, who was coming out of the general store, followed by Sticky Clay.

"Hyah, Bud," greeted Forty Dollar, holding out his hand.

"Ol' Forty Dollar Dion, how are you?" said Bud. "Long time I no see you."

They studied each other for several moments.

"You look all right, Bud," said Forty Dollar.

"Yeah, I'm all right, Forty. It seems good to see you again."

"Thank you, Bud. Say, I want you to meet Silent Slade and Irish O'Day. Gents, this is Bud Bell and Sticky Clay."

"We saw you at the bar before the trouble," said Silent as they shook hands.

"Uh-huh," nodded Sticky. "But we was never introduced."

Bud Bell's eyes never turned from his study of Silent, even when he shook hands with Irish. It was evident to both Silent and Irish that Bud Bell had recognized them by name. Sticky's eyes squinted reflectively as he seemed to try and place them. Silent and Irish had never traveled incognito, even when they were knowingly headed into a troubled spot.

Moolock was a long way from any place where they had operated, and it was not surprising that more men did not recognize them by name.

There came an awkward pause, broken by Sticky Clay.

"We better be getting back to the ranch with this stuff, Bud."

"All right," nodded Bud. "Pleased to have met you gents."

They crossed the street to their horses and rode out of town, while Silent, Irish, and Forty Dollar sauntered down to the office.

"Did you ever know that tall puncher?" asked Clay as he and Bud rode out of town. "Seems like I've heard that name."

"I don't know him," replied Bud slowly, thoughtfully. "But I've heard about him, Sticky. There was a man in the penitentiary, serving time for murder, who told me about him. This convict was part of a gang in Montana and he was the only one to get out alive. Slade sent him to the pen."

"What do you reckon they're doing around here?" queried Sticky.

Bud shook his head slowly. "I don't know. Maybe Allenby has hired him."

"Well, maybe," said Sticky dubiously. "You

never can tell. Still, when you knocked Harry Allenby down, and Hobson and Omaha were coming from the pool table, I seen this tall puncher's hand swinging back toward his gun, and he kinda humped a little. I seen all this out of the corner of my eye. Maybe he's hired by Allenby, but I'm wondering what would have happened if Allenby's gang had started anything."

Bud shook his head and examined his skinned knuckles, which had come in contact with Harry Allenby's teeth.

"I heard," added Sticky Clay, "that Clayton, the cattle-buyer, is going to marry June Allenby."

Bud looked up quickly, but Sticky was looking straight ahead, his Stetson pulled low over his eyes. For several moments, they rode silently.

Bud's thin lips twisted painfully as he finally said:

"Well, she'd sure make him a good wife."

"That side of it is all right," observed Sticky. "She'd make any man a good wife."

"If he was lucky enough to get her," said Bud softly.

Sticky squinted sideways under the protection of his wide hat at Bud, who was gazing unblinkingly at the bobbing ears of his horse.

CHAPTER THREE

Frank Allenby fairly boiled with indignation when Chet Hobson told him what had happened in the Elk Saloon. Harry had refused to come home with Hobson and Omaha. Hobson told Allenby exactly what had transpired, without excusing Harry in any way.

Allenby did not stop to consider that Harry had been a foolish young man; he only saw the disgrace to the Allenby family in having an ex-convict knock his son down in a saloon brawl.

"Why didn't you and Omaha defend him?" he demanded hotly.

Hobson shook his head. "Harry was wrong; and Sticky Clay had every man in the room covered before Harry went down. And Clay will shoot."

"Well, perhaps," grunted Allenby grudgingly. "And Harry wouldn't come home, eh?"

"No."

"He must feel the disgrace keenly." Allenby turned away from Hobson and went into the ranch house.

Hobson squinted after him, shook his head, turned, and sauntered down to the bunkhouse, where Omaha was stretched out on a bunk, reading an old novel.

"How'd he take it?" asked Omaha.

"Rearing straight up," replied Hobson. "I told him that Harry wouldn't come home, and he said that Harry must feel the disgrace keenly."

Omaha said, "'The disgrace keenly,' huh! Didja tell him everything that Harry said?"

"Every word, cowboy."

"He ought to be proud of his offspring."

"That's the hell of it, Omaha—he is!"

June Allenby was in the parlor of the ranch house when her father came in after his talk with Hobson, and she could see that he was greatly perturbed. June was a tall, slender girl, with an unruly crown of soft brown hair above a face that the cowboys of the Moolock Valley swore "has anything beat that ever came over the hills." But June was not vain about her good looks.

Allenby flung himself down in an easy chair that creaked a protest and stared moodily at the well-worn Navajo rug under his feet.

"What has gone wrong now, Pa?" asked June, closing the book she had been reading.

He lifted his head and stared at her.

"Wrong? Everything is wrong. Bud Bell whipped your brother in the Elk Saloon today. Knocked him down like a dog!" Allenby grasped the arms of the chair, as though trying to tear them from their moorings.

June colored slightly and looked away.

"Why did he do it?" she asked calmly.

"Why?" snorted her father. "Possibly Bud Bell thought it would help to pay me back for sending him to prison."

"Don't you know what started it?"

"What difference does that make?" he said.

"Had Harry been drinking?"

"Drinking. He doesn't—"

"Yes, he does, Pa. Omaha told me—"

"Oh, well! They all drink a little. Harry isn't a drinker."

"Perhaps it doesn't take much liquor to make him drunk," suggested June as she stared at her father.

Allenby looked thoughtfully at June for several seconds. He chuckled angrily and got to his feet.

"June, are you trying to defend Bud Bell?" he snapped, his hands resting on his hips.

"No, I—"

"You met him at several dances before—"

"You had him locked up," said June, her eyes snapping. "Yes, I did dance with Bud Bell. He was a gentleman."

"Gentleman, bah!" snorted Allenby. "He stole my cows."

"That's what some say," said June, fingering the book still in her hands. She looked her father squarely in the eye. "You hate Bud and his father!"

"I do!" snapped her father. "I have just cause for feeling that way!"

"You have no real evidence," said June evenly. "It was flimsy evidence that sent Bud to the penitentiary. You know it, but you wanted to get even for things that have happened—things that perhaps could have been caused by others. Oh, yes,

Pa, there are others besides the Bell family that hate you!"

Allenby clenched his fists at his side. He knew his daughter was a fighter like him, but her views of things were different.

"I don't give a hoot who hates me!" snarled the man hotly. "I stand on my rights as a rancher."

"Does that give you the right to lord it over everyone—even your own family?"

"My family?" queried Allenby, his eyes narrowing. "Why did you say that I lord it over my family?"

"After loving yourself, you love Harry," replied June coldly. "You don't give a darn about Mother and me. Oh, don't try to deny it, Pa. I've seen it since I was old enough to have good sense."

Allenby snorted and pawed at the Navajo rug with his boot toe, like a bull preparing to charge. He and June had had their differences, but this was the first time it had come out in the open so bluntly.

"You—you mean to say that I favor Harry?" he demanded.

"Yes, Pa, you do, and you know it," snapped June as she tossed the book aside and got to her feet. "He's a precious little boy as far as you are concerned, and he can do no wrong. You know, deep in your heart, that he's drinking his life away. He'll get himself killed one of these days because he was raised to think and believe that no one can do anything to an Allenby."

Frank Allenby's eyes narrowed, his face turning a pasty white. He was sick to his stomach. No one had ever spoken that way to him before; and he knew that June was right. But he was too stubborn to admit it.

"Then you believe Bud Bell had a right to knock Harry down in the saloon?" he demanded.

"Yes, I do," nodded June. "I know my brother and his mouth, and as long as you won't tell me what happened, I'll suppose that Harry spoke out of turn and got what was coming to him."

She turned on her heel and walked out of the room, going into the kitchen. She could hear her father cursing a blue streak as he stomped his feet on the floor. She stopped just inside the kitchen, a smile of satisfaction on her face.

"Junie," said a voice that caused her to turn. Sitting at the table was Mrs. Allenby, a sweet gray-haired little woman, who looked up at her daughter. "I heard you."

"I'm sorry, Mother, but I couldn't help it."

The elderly woman nodded understandingly. "Frank always has the last word—until this time," she said softly.

"He'll still have it," smiled June as she sat down at the table and looked at her mother. "He'll try to get even with me. I know him. No one can cross him. But, Mother, I feel I've grown up. I'll be ready for him, for anything he might try."

"What about Bud Bell?" asked her mother, her eyes searching her daughter's face.

"He has always been nice to me," replied June. "I haven't seen him since he came home. We had a lot of fun together. He—he never seemed like a cattle rustler, Mother."

"Are you sure about Harry—his drinking?"

June nodded. "Yes, I am, Mother. He's drunk most of the time. That's why you see very little of him. He only comes here in the mornings after he's sobered up. You never see him at night because he's too drunk to put in an appearance."

"How can he drink that much on forty dollars a month?"

"I don't know, but I have an idea," replied June. "You just relax and don't worry about anything. Maybe Pa will think things over and see them from a different light."

"I doubt that. After thirty years, I know him fairly well."

They heard a vehicle rattle over the hard ground outside, and June stepped to the kitchen window and looked outside. Mrs. Allenby watched her daughter, a smile on her face.

"Who's there, dear?" she asked.

"Clayton with a stranger," replied June, turning away from the window. "I'll be in my room. I have no desire to talk with Ed Clayton."

Frank Allenby stepped out on the front porch just as Clayton and the stranger climbed out of the buggy. The stranger was of medium size, dark features, and had a small black mustache. He was dressed in dark clothes.

"Mr. Allenby, meet Mr. Seeley—Jim Seeley," said Clayton.

The two men shook hands jerkily. Clayton took a big suitcase from the buggy and placed it on the porch.

"Kind of a pretty place you've got here, Mr. Allenby," said Seeley, glancing around. "I never seen a cow ranch with so much paint before. You believe in duding up the place, don't you?"

"Just because it's a cattle ranch, there is no need of living like savages," replied Allenby.

"Mr. Allenby is several jumps ahead of the rest of the country," declared Clayton. "He's progressive. His ranch house is as fine as a home in the city, and I'll defy you to find a broken board, loose post, or a loose wire on the place."

Seeley laughed. "I'm not going to look."

"Well, you couldn't find it," declared Allenby proudly. "I've seen to it all myself. Do you intend to stay right here?"

"Why not?" asked Seeley. "I'm working for you now."

"Well, I'm glad to have you," said Allenby. "And when I hire a man, I want him where I can see that he's on the job all the time. Come on in and meet the family."

Seeley shot a side glance at Clayton, who was trying to suppress a smile, and they followed Allenby into the house.

"Now, who do you reckon that is?" queried Omaha, who was looking out of the bunkhouse window and saw the men going into the house.

Hobson joined him and looked at the stranger.

"That must be the private investigator that Clayton sent for," he said dryly. "Allenby has had the detective idea for some time, it seems. He lost faith in the Cattle Association and had some words with the secretary, who promised to get him a first-class cow detective. But it seems that Allenby didn't ante high enough to get his man. Or maybe there was some other problem."

"He wouldn't make the ante too high," agreed Omaha, turning away from the window. "I don't like to appear disloyal, but personally I think that Allenby is so stingy that he takes out his false teeth at night to save the wear and tear on his mouth."

Omaha went back to his novel, while Chet Hobson sat down to play a game of solitaire. The foreman's mind was thinking about the new addition to the crew and how should he treat a cow detective. His thoughts were interrupted when Harry Allenby came into the bunkhouse. His nose was badly swollen, as was his upper lip; but he was well loaded with liquor, and if he had been disgraced, he did not show it.

"Who's at the house?" he asked thickly, trying to point in the direction of the ranch house.

"Clayton and a stranger," grunted Hobson.

"Who's the stranger?"

"I don't know," Hobson said.

"That so?" Harry sat down on a bunk and looked owlishly at Omaha, who grinned behind his book.

"He's a detective, sonny," said Omaha. "He's come here to save your papa's little cowlets."

"That so?" Harry blinked thoughtfully. "Is he a good one?"

"Sure is," said Omaha. "He's the jigger that found the Lost Chord, if you know what that is."

"Well, I dunno. Ol' man up at the house?" Harry asked.

"Yeah, he's there. If I was you, I'd doctor up that nose and lip, Harry. You're a mite messed up, if you ask me."

"You better crawl into bed and sleep it off," suggested Hobson, without looking up from his cards. "Don't let your family see you drunk."

"That so?" Harry stumbled over to a mirror and squinted at himself with one eye shut.

"I'm a sweet-lookin' lily, that's a cinch," he concluded.

He came back to the center of the room, as though the sight of himself had sobered him a little.

"I'm goin' back to town," he decided.

"You better stay right here," said Hobson. "Shuck off your clothes and go to bed."

"Not if I can get away without the folks seein' me."

He opened the door cautiously, then peered out for several moments before going out and heading for the stable. As he stepped into the stable, he stopped short. Leaning against the stall where he had left his horse was his sister, June. He started to turn around, but she stopped him.

"Just a minute, big brother!" she snapped.

"Huh? Whatcha doin' out here, Junie?"

"I saw you ride in and sneaked down here," replied June, her eyes drilling into his. "You're a drunken bum, Harry! And you want to go back and drink more, eh?"

"That's my business."

"Yes, I know it is, but I'm on the warpath, big brother. I told Pa off, and now I'm telling you off." June's voice cut into Harry like a sliver of ice. "You drink too much. You better stop, or we'll be burying you because your mouth will get you killed. You don't know how to act like a man. You think that the more you drink, the bigger man it makes you—but you're wrong! Dead wrong! Think of Mother. She worships you. Do you want to hurt her?"

Harry blinked drunkenly, shook his head, and stepped forward, shoving June away from the stall. He got the reins and pulled his horse out of the stall while June leaned against the wall and watched him mount and ride out of the stable.

Omaha was at the bunkhouse window watching, and when he saw Harry ride away, he turned and looked at Hobson.

"Danged fool kid," said Hobson.

"Yeah." Omaha nodded. "He's a fool, all right, I suppose. Still, he's old enough to know what he wants. I blame Allenby more than I do the kid. He barely pays Harry a cowpuncher's wages."

Someone was talking just outside the door, so Omaha went back to the window and looked out at Swan River Smith and Forty Dollar Dion, who had just ridden up to the bunkhouse from the rear of the ranch.

"The law has found us, Chet," Omaha said as he threw the door open. "Howdy, officers," he called. "Get down and appear amiable."

"Hello, Omaha," said Swan River as he dismounted. "Is Allenby at home? I mean, 'Mr.' Allenby."

Omaha grinned widely and pointed toward the house, where Allenby, Clayton, and Seeley had come out on the porch.

"Who's the dude?" asked Forty Dollar.

"Don't know," replied Omaha. "He came out with Ed Clayton."

Clayton got into the buggy and drove away and, after a few minutes of conversation, Allenby and Seeley came down to the bunkhouse.

Allenby did not introduce Seeley to any of them, but spoke directly to the sheriff:

"Something you wanted, Mr. Smith?"

"Nothing I exactly wanted, Mr. Allenby," said the sheriff. "It was kind of in regard to your loss of last night. In reply, I can say that I ain't been able to find any clues—yet. In your talk this morning, you kind of hinted that you suspected somebody of purloining your cows, and if you ain't got nothing else to do right now, I'd kind of like to have you explain your suspicions to me. Sincerely yours, Swan River Smith, sheriff of Moolock."

Swan River had intoned the whole statement, as though dictating a letter, and Allenby's ears reddened quickly. Omaha smothered a grin, but Forty Dollar Dion laughed outright. Allenby glared angrily at Forty Dollar, but that worthy did not mind.

"Are you trying to be smart, or just funny?" Allenby asked Smith.

"It's all in the point of view," replied Swan River evenly.

"All right," Allenby said viciously. "As far as my losses are concerned, you may just forget them. I'm not asking any assistance from the sheriff's office, and I don't care to have you volunteer any. I hope you understand what I mean."

"Hell, you didn't leave many loopholes for a mistake to crawl through," said Swan River. "But your likes and dislikes don't mean a thing to me, Allenby. I'm sheriff of this county, and I want to tell you—"

"Pardon me, but you can't tell me anything," said Allenby.

"That's the trouble with you," said Swan River slowly. "You think that you're a tin god around here, Allenby. Another thing you might do without any advice from me—and that is to look after that half-baked son of yours.

"He came danged near getting what was coming to him today, when he opened his mouth too wide. You've brought him up, Allenby, to think too damned much of the name Allenby. Now I'm telling this to you for your own good. And you might preach it to him and practice a little of it yourself. When you've got some evidence that'll hold in court, let me look at it. In the meantime, think what you please, but keep your mouth shut. I hate to conduct coroners' inquests. *Adios.*"

The two officers mounted and rode away without another word while Allenby gasped with wrath. Omaha stepped back into the bunkhouse, where he could laugh in safety, while Allenby spluttered and told the wide world what he thought of Sheriff Swan River Smith.

"That blasted little runt!" he snorted. "I—I'll show him what I can do, blast his hide!"

"He's still the law," said Hobson.

Allenby glared at his foreman.

"I'll take the law into my own hands," he snorted.

Seeley looked from Allenby to Hobson, slightly embarrassed. Allenby noticed Seeley and realized he had not introduced him.

"Jim Seeley, this is my foreman, Chet Hobson," he said.

The two men shook hands. He did not tell Hobson what Seeley's business was, but added, "He'll be living in the bunkhouse with you boys."

"That's fine," grunted Hobson. "There's several empty bunks, so take your pick."

Allenby turned to his foreman.

"We're going to town, Chet," he said. "Hitch up the team, please."

Hobson hurried to the stable. The two men stood in the doorway until he had the team hitched to the buggy. Then they climbed in and drove away.

Hobson sauntered back to the bunkhouse. Omaha looked up at the foreman.

"Probably going down to tell his son that the fatted calf is almost ready for the barbecue," said Omaha.

"More likely going down to save his little lamb from the slaughter," corrected Hobson. "Me and you better fix a new lock on this bunkhouse door, Omaha. The next thing we know, somebody will steal us."

CHAPTER FOUR

For the next two days Moolock was devoid of excitement. Silent Slade and Irish O'Day spent their time loafing around the Elk where Silent had fun playing card tricks on many. They made the acquaintance of several cowboys, but had not tried to secure work. Silent felt that things were too quiet and suggested to Irish that they move on, but Irish demurred.

"You go if you want to, but I still want my horse," snorted Irish.

"I want mine, too, but so far we've drawn nothing but blanks," said Silent.

"Let's wait," suggested Irish. "Something tells me that Moolock is a good place for us to be, Silent. The poker games ain't too avaricious, they put up good food, and I ain't found a bug in that hotel. You don't find many places as good as this, cowboy."

"That's all right with me," grinned Silent, who really wanted to stay for a while.

Swan River Smith and Forty Dollar Dion had scoured the country, trying to see what they could see; but there was no trace of Allenby's three hundred Herefords. The express company had flooded Swan River with correspondence regarding the train robbery, but as yet they had offered no reward.

Silent and Irish sauntered down to the sheriff's office after dinner at the restaurant. They found the sheriff going through some correspondence while Forty Dollar was half asleep on the cot. Swan River glanced up as they came in, but Forty Dollar merely grunted.

"More correspondence?" queried Silent.

"Yeah," nodded the sheriff, looking up. "What do they expect from me? I marked them robbers off my slate as soon as they got into Bearpaw. I'd like to see you fellows get your broncs back, though."

"Me, too," said Irish. "They were the best pair of animals that ever wore a saddle. How that roan of mine could fly."

"I thought you lost a horse," said Forty Dollar, opening one eye.

"Fast, man, he was fast," said Irish.

"Uh-huh," grunted Forty Dollar. "Bet it could run a mile in spite of—"

"Just about twice that fast," said Irish. "It was one really fine horse, noted for endurance. It was the horse that old emperor or something or other meant when he yelled that he'd trade his kingdom for a horse. Yes, sir, I'm sure pining a lot for that hunk of coyote bait."

"Pining is right," said Silent, shaking his head.

"He turned down a second piece of pie this noon. I'm worried about him."

"Don't need to be," said Forty Dollar. "He'll be all right soon as he learns to tell the truth."

The sheriff shoved the correspondence away from him and got to his feet, hitching up his pants and adjusting his gun belt.

"Enough's enough," he snorted.

"I feel the same way," said Silent.

Irish squinted at Forty Dollar, who looked around. "Going to stay here?" asked Irish.

"Not me," replied the deputy, swinging his feet off the cot and standing up.

He and Irish followed the sheriff and Silent out to the boardwalk.

As they all started across the street toward the Elk, two riders swung into the main street, leading two horses. It was Jack Merton, owner of the Arrowhead outfit, and one of his men, Pete Sepulveda.

Silent and Irish looked quickly at each other as they recognized the two horses that were coming along behind Merton and Sepulveda. There was no mistaking Silent's tall bay and Irish's hammer-headed roan. Merton waved to the sheriff as he swung into the hitchrack in front of the Elk and dismounted. Sepulveda tied up the two horses they had led into town.

The sheriff's group stepped up on the boardwalk in front of the hitchrack and stopped, eyeing the horses. Swan River squinted at the two horses, then half turned and looked at Silent and Irish.

"Seen anybody that lost two horses?" asked Merton, a tall, well-built cowboy with a pleasant face. "These two were camped at my stable this morning; so I brought them in, Sheriff.

One's branded with a JK and the other with a Triangle-6. They don't show in my register book."

"They belong to us," said Silent.

"Them's the two, eh?" grunted Forty Dollar. "Is them the two critters you been wailing about? Well, well, well! Huh!"

"What about it?" asked Merton interestedly.

"Well." Swan River scratched his head thoughtfully. "It ain't ready for explanation, Jack. You just take my word for it that the horses belong to these gents, will you?"

"Anything you say, Swan River." Merton grinned and hitched up his chaps.

"That's fine of you," said the sheriff, and then he proceeded to introduce Silent and Irish to Merton and Sepulveda. They all adjourned into the Elk Saloon, and as they were having a drink, another rider came into town.

It was not difficult to see that this rider's veins carried a certain percentage of Indian blood. He was nearly six feet tall, about forty-five years of age, and had a deeply lined face and prominent cheekbones. And he wore a beaded calf vest.

He looked over the horses at the hitchrack, especially the two strange ones, before dismounting. Seemingly satisfied with his inspection, he tied his sorrel horse at the rack, adjusted his belt, and strode into the saloon.

"Well, well, here comes Joe Bass," exclaimed Swan River as the newcomer approached the bar. "How are you, Joe?"

"Pretty good, you bet," laughed Bass. "Hello, Forty Dollar. Hello, Merton. How are you? By golly, there's Pete Sepulveda!"

"Have a drink," invited Swan River.

"Sure, I drink whisky. I'm pretty dry these days."

When the additional drink came, Swan River introduced Silent and Irish to Joe Bass, who grunted and grinned widely.

"I see two strange horses at the rack," he stated. "I don't know the brands; so I suppose strangers are here. You ride bareback, eh?"

"Well, here's regards," said Silent, ignoring Bass's question. He knew that the sheriff did not want to explain about the lost horses. Bass noticed the evasion and raised his brows slightly; but he drank his liquor and did not bring up the subject again.

"You don't happen to know of somebody that wants to hire a couple of good punchers, do you?" asked Silent, speaking to Merton.

Merton shook his head and motioned to the bartender to get busy.

"No, I don't," he said. "I've got a full crew. Maybe Joe needs some help."

"Not much," replied Bass quickly. "I got too much help now. Pinon Meade and Lem Elder sit in the shade all the time."

"Must take a lot of shade for the three of you," observed Swan River.

Joe Bass laughed loudly, nodding excitedly. "By golly, that's right!" he exploded. "I'm lazy, too. Swan River knows. Some cattlemen work all the time. Look at Allenby. He make new fence, paint it pretty, paint the house. He's rich. Joe Bass let ranch go to blazes. He's poor.

"Allenby work all the time; worry, too, I guess. He's a fool. Joe Bass never work much, never worry. No time. He's a fool, too. Let's have another drink, eh? Drink to two fools."

"Allenby wouldn't appreciate that," laughed Merton. "He sure thinks he's a wise man. Personally, I think Joe Bass is right. Allenby is full of hate."

"Danged right he is," agreed Forty Dollar. "Any old time a man says that Frank Allenby is a fool, I'll agree with him."

"What about Allenby losing three hundred Herefords?" asked Merton. "Was that a fact?"

"You ask Allenby," laughed Forty Dollar.

"He came by the Arrowhead and told me about it," said Merton. "I thought perhaps he was shooting off his mouth. He had a stranger with him. Allenby never introduced him to any of us."

"Afraid we might take him away," laughed Sepulveda. "He didn't look like much. Don't think he was worth taking away—even from Allenby."

The bartender squinted past the men toward the doorway. Swan River saw him and turned. A towheaded youngster was coming into the room, walking carefully as if he were stepping on eggs. He glanced wildly about, his eyes wide with wonder.

"What do you want, sonny?" asked the bartender.

"I—I want the sheriff," said the boy.

"Me?" asked Swan River, setting his glass down on the bar. "What do you want?"

"You—you better come out here." The lad turned and fairly ran out of the saloon.

"Maybe I better," said Swan River, and he was followed by everyone but Forty Dollar, who had had a little too much to drink to understand what was taking place.

The boy was on the boardwalk, pointing excitedly toward the hitchrack in front of the general store, where a man sat drunkenly on a horse, reins dragging.

"That looks danged funny!" exclaimed the sheriff, and they all hurried across the street to the man.

He was roped to the saddle with a long lariat. And tied to the rope, where it circled the man's neck, was a fairly fresh cowhide.

It was Jim Seeley, Allenby's detective. His face was gray as ashes, except where it was caked with blood. There was also blood all over his shirt. It appeared that the man had been shot in the head and in the body. Silent took out his knife and cut the ropes, while the others lowered him to the walk.

He groaned painfully and collapsed. Swan River sent men after the doctor. Silent spread out the cowhide. It had been taken from a Hereford two-year-old, and the brand on the right shoulder was a Half-Circle Cross.

"Does anybody know him?" asked Swan River.

"He's the fellow that was with Allenby at the Arrowhead," replied Merton.

"Yeah," said Sepulveda. "That's the man, all right. What did he run into?"

"Rustlers," grunted Silent as he studied the man on the ground. "It kind of looks like he'd collected the hide of one of Allenby's missing Herefords. He got creased along the head, and it looks like there might be a bullet in his right shoulder, which made him lose quite some blood."

The youngster came running back down the walk and pushed his way through the crowd that surrounded the fallen Seeley.

"I got the doctor," he said, yanking at Swan River's shirt sleeve. "I got there first before anyone else!"

"Good," grunted Swan River as the sixtyish doctor shoved his way through the crowd and knelt beside Seeley. He made a quick examination, then turned to the sheriff, adjusting his eyeglasses.

"Get him down to my house pronto," he snapped, getting to his feet and dusting off the knees of his gray trousers. He watched intently as some men secured a blanket and placed the injured Seeley on it. Several men volunteered to carry the man down to the doctor's house, so Swan River let them go. He picked up the cowhide and took it down the street to his office where he draped it across the little hitchrack.

"What do you make of it, Slade?" he asked seriously. "Why would anybody shoot this man, tie him to a saddle, and send him back with a cowhide?"

"You want my opinion, Swan River?"

"Yes," said the sheriff.

"Well, I haven't got one. It kind of looks to me like somebody was trying to take a slap at Mr. Allenby."

Swan River sighed deeply. All this was only piling misery up for him.

"I suppose I've got to make an arrest pretty soon," he said slowly, looking keenly at Silent and Irish. "I ain't got a bit of evidence to make it on; but the arrow points mostly one way. Still, I don't know."

They then went into the office. Swan River was perturbed, and he showed it by pacing back and forth while Irish leaned against the doorway and Silent sat on a corner of the desk.

"I really don't know where to turn, Slade," the sheriff said, still pacing. "This confuses my mind. Everything's peaceful for so long. Then comes the train robbery, with the robbers stealing your horses, the stealing of the three hundred Herefords of Allenby's, and now this. Thank heaven you've got your horses back."

"We're grateful, but we'd sure like to know who took them," said Irish.

Swan River squinted at Irish, then turned to Silent.

"Will this keep you here for a while?" he asked. "You said you were only staying until you found your broncs."

"We're here for a spell," said Silent as he thought of Seeley. "It's getting interesting now, Sheriff."

"Interesting—hell!" snorted Swan River as he turned and walked to the doorway beside Irish and looked out on the street. Hank and Bud Bell were dismounting at the Elk Saloon.

"There's old Hank Bell," said the sheriff, half turning to Silent, who slid off the corner of the desk and joined Swan River and Irish at the doorway.

Hank Bell was a little man who carried his right arm sharply bent at the elbow. He and Bud came across the street and entered the general store.

"That pinto and gray belong to old Hank," said Swan River softly. "Bud rides the pinto."

"You still got them in your stable in back?" asked Silent.

"Sure thing. When they start inquiring about lost horses, it'll be time enough for me to do my talking," replied the sheriff, rubbing his chin thoughtfully. "Nobody except us and Forty know about them."

Silent nodded as he stepped past the others and walked slowly up the boardwalk toward the general store. He was curious to see Hank Bell, so he went inside the store. Bud was buying some cartridges from the proprietor, who was telling him about the stranger who had been shot.

Old Hank seemed indifferent to the telling, but Silent could see that the man was actually not missing a word of it.

He was of the old school of cattlemen. He was small, wiry of frame, thin faced, his white hair reaching to his collar. His eyes were as hard as agate, but there were enough grin wrinkles around them to prove that old Hank Bell was not always serious. His right arm was crippled in such a way that he was unable to reach below his waist; and Silent noticed that the old man wore his holster on the left side, tied down.

Regular old wolf, Silent told himself. Taught himself to draw and shoot left-handed.

The proprietor had almost finished telling his story, and a ghost of a smile flitted across old Hank's lips when the man spoke about the Half-Circle Cross cowhide that was hanging from the man's neck.

Bud turned and nodded to Silent. He spoke softly to his father, who shot a quick glance at Silent. Pete Sepulveda came into the store and spoke to Silent.

"That fellow was shot twice, Slade, like you said. The one creased his head and won't amount to much; but the other went plumb through him. He was shot from behind. The doctor don't know whether it'll kill him or not. Do you know who he is?"

"Nope." Silent shook his head. "Somebody said he was staying at the Allenby ranch."

"Allenby just drove into town. I saw him as I came in here," said Pete.

Silent walked to the doorway and looked out on

the street. Allenby and his daughter, June, were in the buckboard, stopped in the middle of the street, talking with two men who had just come from the doctor's house. As Silent watched them, Allenby whipped up his team and went toward the doctor's place.

Bud completed his purchases and walked across the street to the Elk Saloon, followed by his father, who gave Silent a searching glance as he went past.

"He's a tough old pelican," declared Sepulveda. "Don't think he's been in a shooting scrape since he got his arm busted; but I'm betting that he really knows how to shoot left-handed. Them old jiggers shoot first and talk afterwards."

"Plenty tough, eh?"

"Uh-huh! Old Hank used to be awful fast with a gun. He had a funny way of getting his gun, Slade. He'd kind of swing his hand behind the holster—like a fellow might swing back his hand when walking and on the back swing he pulled and shot all at once. I don't know how he did it. I've tried to do it. No good. They tell me he showed Bud how to do it; but I ain't never seen Bud have to shoot—yet."

They stepped out on the walk where Merton and Irish joined them. Irish had met Merton up the street near the doctor's place, and they came down the walk together.

"Allenby is throwing a fit," declared Merton. "He acts like he was the one that got shot. I asked him who this fellow was, and he told me it was none of my business—which it wasn't. I've heard a lot of profanity, but Allenby's got them all skinned."

"Not in front of his daughter?" asked Silent.

"No, she didn't stay; she drove over to the post office."

Swan River and Joe Bass were coming down the street, but they turned into the White Horse Saloon.

"I'll buy a drink," offered Sepulveda, and Irish accepted.

But Silent shook his head. "Thank you just the same, Sepulveda. Maybe I'll join you later."

Irish and Sepulveda followed Merton to the Elk Saloon, leaving Silent cogitating over certain things.

Bud Bell came out of the saloon as Merton, Irish, and Sepulveda went in. He declined their invitation to drink and came back over to the store for something he'd forgotten.

"How is everything, Slade?" he asked as he went past.

"Oh, kind of interesting, Bell," smiled Silent.

June Allenby was coming down the street, carrying some packages in her hands. It was the first time that Silent had seen her close, and he was forced to agree with Forty Dollar Dion that June Allenby was a "dinger."

It was not like Silent to stare at a lady, but he did. In fact, he was so interested in her that he did not hear Bud Bell come out of the store. June lifted her eyes from the boardwalk and looked straight past Silent, who turned his head and discovered Bud Bell behind him.

They had both stopped and were staring at each other. Silent wished that he was on the opposite side of the street instead of almost directly between these two. Then Bud stepped to the edge of the walk, as though to start across the street; but the girl halted him with a motion of her hand.

"Bud," she said, "aren't you going to even say hello?"

Bud's hand went uncertainly to his hat, but his eyes shifted from June and glanced quickly around.

"Yes'm, I reckon that wouldn't hurt anybody, and I didn't want to hurt you."

He stepped off the walk and headed swiftly across the street. Silent watched June's face as she followed him with her eyes until he went back into the Elk Saloon. Silent wanted to speak to her, to tell her that he would help to straighten things out, but he was tongue-tied. Perhaps she read his intentions in his eyes as she passed him and went into the store.

She loves Bud Bell! Silent told himself wonderingly. Can you beat that? This is sure a queer world. And in spite of all the trouble Frank Allenby has caused Bud Bell, I'm betting that Bud Bell loves Allenby's daughter. He said he didn't want to hurt her. I wonder if he meant— oh, well, let's see.

Silent hooked his thumb over the waistband of his jeans and considered the situation for a space of time. His eyes shifted to the two horses at the hitchrack.

By golly, I've got to fix a place for them broncs, he told himself. And this is as good a time as any, I reckon.

He turned on his heel and went slowly down the street.

Silent was barely out of sight when Frank Allenby came back from the doctor's house. His face was black with anger and his hands were clenched at his sides as he strode along. Near the door of the Elk Saloon he stopped and studied the

horses at the various hitchracks. He saw the two
horses that Hank Bell and his son had ridden.

"Both here," muttered Allenby, half aloud.
"Well, I've stood enough! I'll get it straightened
out once and for all time!" He turned, grimacing,
as though he tasted wormwood and gall, and went
into the saloon.

Swan River Smith and Joe Bass saw him cross
the street in front of the White Horse Saloon. They
lost no time in crowding into the Elk behind
Allenby. He was standing in the middle of the
room, looking at Hank Bell, who was standing at
the bar with Irish and Pete Sepulveda. He did
not notice that the sheriff was behind him.

Bud Bell was sitting beside a card table, looking
at an old newspaper, but now his eyes shifted to
Allenby.

"I've stood about all I'm going to, Bell," Allenby
said to old Hank Bell in a shaking voice.

Hank Bell turned slowly, his left hand swinging
back of him, as though to shove him away from
the bar.

"Look out!" whispered Pete Sepulveda, who
knew what that movement meant.

Allenby was not a gunman. It was doubtful if
he could hit Hank Bell at that distance; but his
anger had made him forget all caution. He wanted
to crush this little, crooked-armed old man. But
Hank Bell was not going to fight him. He stood
there, poised easily, his left hand splayed out behind him.

But before anything more could be said, Swan
River Smith butted Allenby with his left shoulder,
while his right hand snatched Allenby's gun from
its holster. The jolt turned the big man halfway
around and he struck at the little sheriff; but Swan

River easily dodged the blow and stepped between Allenby and Hank Bell.

"And that'll be about all of this show," said the sheriff calmly. "If you fellows want to go gunning for each other, you better go out on the flat somewhere."

"I wasn't gunning for anybody," said old Hank slowly. "But I hate to disappoint anybody when they ask me for trouble."

"That's all right, Hank." Swan River turned to Allenby. "Someday, Allenby, you'll make a mistake. And it'll probably be the kind of mistake that a man only makes once in his life. I don't blame you for being mad, but you ought to use some judgment."

"What was this to you?" demanded Allenby hotly. "You had no right to interfere with my business! Give me back my gun!"

Swan River grinned and shoved the gun inside the waistband of his pants.

"When you get ready to go home, I'll just do that," he said. "I'm kind of responsible for the wear and tear on Moolock, you know."

"You're responsible for a lot of things," sneered Allenby. "I came to town to get a little more information from you, Smith. This morning I had a little talk with a man named Pierson. He's from Tecoma. He told me a little story about you being at Tecoma the other night—the evening of the day that the express robbery was pulled off.

"He told me about two men whose horses were stolen by the bandits, and he told me about a pinto and a gray that were left at the hitchrack. The pinto had a coal black head. Pierson saw the brands, too. What about it, Sheriff?"

Swan River scowled. He realized that there was

nothing more he could do to keep that evidence under cover. Hank Bell and Bud were looking straight at each other, and now Bud got slowly to his feet.

"Take it easy," Irish advised softly.

Bud flashed a glance at him, as though wondering why Irish had said that.

"Well, what about it?" asked Allenby triumphantly.

He felt that he was putting the screws to Swan River Smith, and he knew that it was not welcome news to the Bell family.

"What about it?" queried Swan River vacantly. "Huh! Pierson told you this, did he?"

"Yes, he did. Would he have any reason to lie?"

"No, I don't reckon he would, Allenby."

"What about the pinto and the gray?" asked Bud Bell wonderingly.

Swan River pursed his lips as he shook his head slowly.

"You've got those horses," declared Allenby. "You've had them ever since that night."

Swan River did not deny it. Peter Sepulveda and Jack Merton looked at Irish.

"That's how you lost your two horses, eh?" said Merton.

Irish ignored the question.

"Are they in your stable or at the livery barn?" asked Allenby.

"You might find out by looking," said Swan River.

"All right!" snapped Allenby. "You know as well as I do that those two horses belong to Hank Bell. Now, what are you going to do about it?"

"Do about it?" parroted Swan River.

"Yes! Are you going to let them escape while

we go to look at the evidence?" snarled Allenby.

Swan River squinted at Hank and Bud.

"Are you?" Allenby asked.

Old Hank shook his head and said:

"I'd rather fight than run, Swan River. Suppose we go with you."

"That's a hell of a way to run your office!" exploded Allenby. "Some of these days—"

"Suppose you stay here, Allenby," suggested Swan River.

"No! All I want is a square deal. We'll go to the livery barn first."

"Suit yourself."

Allenby whirled and led the way out of the Elk, followed by Swan River, Hank and Bud Bell, Irish, Merton, and Sepulveda. They all trooped to the livery stable. It did not take them long to find that the two horses were not there.

"Then you've got them in your stable!" snorted Allenby as he glared at the sheriff.

"Let's look," suggested Swan River.

Then they went to the sheriff's stable behind his office, where they found Silent, busily currying the tall bay. In the next stall stood the roan, belonging to Irish, and in the two other stalls stood Swan River's sorrel and Forty Dollar's buckskin.

Silent looked curiously at the crowd but did not cease grooming his horse. Swan River leaned against the doorway and rubbed his chin, while the rest of the crowd looked around blankly and came outside.

"I—I hope you're satisfied," said Swan River chokingly.

"Satisfied, hell!" snorted Allenby. He no longer had the triumphant look on his face of a few minutes prior.

Old Hank scratched his head foolishly and motioned to Bud.

"You don't want us for anything more, do you?" Old Hank said to Swan River.

"Shucks, no," said the sheriff. "I reckon everybody's satisfied."

"I hope so," grunted Old Hank. "C'mon, Bud."

They started walking back through the alley, leaving Allenby staring after them, his lips working painfully. He turned to the sheriff.

"What crooked work is this?" he demanded hotly. "You just the same as admitted that you had those horses."

"I didn't admit nothing," denied Swan River. "I was willing to prove that I didn't."

Allenby looked at Merton and Sepulveda, grunted, pulled the brim of his hat low over his eyes, and stalked down the alley. Merton and Sepulveda chuckled, looked at the sheriff, and grinned.

"Damn him!" snorted Merton. "It did me good to see him crawl some. He thinks he's too good for all of us. Did you have those horses, Swan River?"

The sheriff grinned and shrugged his shoulders as he motioned toward the inside of the stable.

"You saw, didn't you?"

Merton nodded. "C'mon, Pete, let's get a drink before we head for home."

Irish had gone to work on his horse and Silent continued in his effort to clean up his bay. Swan River came into the stable and watched the two cowboys work on their horses.

"I thought they had you, Swan River," said Irish, pausing to clean his currycomb. "You could have knocked me down with a straw."

"Yeah, I felt the same way about it." Swan River looked at Silent questioningly, but the tall cowboy's face was serious.

For several minutes there was nothing but the swish of the currycombs to break the silence.

Finally, Silent stepped back, looked the bay over carefully, and threw the comb into a box against the wall. He walked to the door and looked out as he brushed off his shirt.

"Slade," said Swan River softly. "Did you know that Pierson had talked with Allenby?"

"Pierson?"

"Yeah. He's the fellow who runs the saloon in Tecoma. Did you know that Pierson told Allenby about those two horses—the pinto and the gray one?"

"No, I didn't know it. We needed a place to put our broncs, and I didn't feel like paying a livery stable to keep them."

Swan River took a deep breath and looked at Irish, who had ceased work while Silent was talking.

"And that's about all you'll ever get out of him," Irish said knowingly.

"Well." Swan River sighed with satisfaction. "That's enough for me. Maybe we're all wrong, I don't know. Anyway, I thank you, Silent. It saved me from a lot of explaining."

"You're welcome, Sheriff," said Silent.

He was thinking of a girl who wanted a boy to say hello to her, a boy who was afraid that even a hello from him might harm her.

"This is a hell of a world!" he grunted thoughtfully.

"It sure is," agreed Swan River. "We don't ask

to get in, get trouble while we're here, and get out
because we can't help ourselves. My old pa used
to say—"

"Eat a lot of green vegetables, keep your mouth
shut, and your gun cocked—and you'll live a long
time," said Irish. "How close do you follow that
advice?"

"Well," grinned the sheriff, "I keep my gun
cocked quite a lot of the time. I figure that's what
they call a necessary thing of life—anyway around
here."

CHAPTER FIVE

June Allenby stood at her bedroom window the following morning and watched her father drive away in his buggy. She was dressed in jeans and riding boots. She turned from the window and went to her bed where she picked up a tan Stetson. Then she hurried out of the room.

In the kitchen she found her mother and the Chinese cook going over the daily menu. Her mother turned and looked at her.

"Where are you going, Junie?" she asked.

"I thought I'd like to ride out into the hills," said June. "It's a beautiful day."

"That might do you good," Mrs. Allenby said with a smile. "But be careful, my dear."

"I'll be careful." June smiled back as she crossed the room and went out the rear door.

Hobson and Omaha had ridden away from the ranch prior to Allenby's departure, so June went

to the corral and selected her own horse, a bay
mare, and saddled the animal herself. Then she
mounted with ease and rode off.

June had a destination in mind as she swung
the bay eastward, taking her time. She looked over
the country and checked the cattle as any cowboy
would do. Finally, she came down a slight slope
to a road which went south to the small town of
White Eagle. She crossed the road and swung up
into some low foothills, winding around an old
cattle trail that she hadn't ridden for two years.

Crossing a dry riverbed, she swung off to her
right and onto a low mesa where she stopped. From
there she could look out over the valley, but she
wasn't interested in the valley. Her eyes were riv-
eted on a cluster of buildings below her, not too
far away: the HB ranch house, bunkhouse, and
stable. She leaned forward in her saddle as she
studied the place.

It was some time before she saw signs of life
around the HB. A man came from the bunkhouse
and went into the house. June was sure that was
Sticky Clay. She waited a while, and then two men
came out of the house and went to the stable. They
saddled some horses and rode away, going toward
Moolock. June was sure that it was old Hank Bell
and Sticky. That only left Bud Bell to be accounted
for.

June straightened in her saddle as she saw Bud
Bell come out of the house and go to the stable.
She spurred her horse down the mesa toward the
ranch house.

Bud Bell saddled his horse and was leading
it from the stable when he stopped short. June
Allenby was riding into the ranch yard. He

dropped the reins from his fingers and squinted at her as she drew up in front of the stable door.

"What are you doing here?" he asked, a puzzled expression on his face.

"I just had to see you, Bud," replied June. "I heard what happened yesterday, and I want to say that I'm sorry Pa got so angry!"

"You feel sorry for him, not me," said Bud, shoving his Stetson back from his head. "He always talks too much, June."

"I know." She nodded. "But I wanted you to know how I felt about it."

"You wanted me to know, eh?" grunted Bud. "Why, June?"

"Well, I—I just wanted you to know, that's all."

"I sure appreciate it," grinned Bud. "But you took a big chance coming out here to see an ex-convict."

"I wished you wouldn't say that," said June, shaking her head.

"Why care about me?" asked Bud. "I understand you're going to marry Ed Clayton."

June gasped and shook her head.

"No, I'm not," she said sharply. "Who told you?"

"I just heard it in town," replied Bud, not wanting to implicate Sticky in the matter. "Isn't it true?"

"No," replied June. "I can't stand the man."

Bud smiled and relaxed a little. "That's the best news I've heard since I came back," he said.

June smiled. "I was afraid that you had changed," she said.

"Prisons do change one," said Bud, hanging his head slightly, looking at the toes of his boots. "But I hope I haven't changed that much."

"I hope not," smiled June. "It's too bad our fathers can't be human and forget this bickering."

"It's bad, Junie," he said. "I paid the price for something that I never did, and I'll always carry that prison mark against me. My pa has never done anything wrong, either. Because Ronald Winter felt the way he did about us taking over this land, your father believed him and resented us. In fact, he hates us."

"Hate is a terrible thing," sighed June as she lifted her reins. "Well, I wanted you to know how I felt, Bud."

"You've lit up my day," smiled Bud. "Can I ride a ways with you?"

"I don't see why not," smiled June.

Bud turned, picked up his fallen reins, and vaulted into his saddle. Then they rode out of the yard side by side, going the way June had come.

They rode across the dry riverbed and swung up the low hills in silence, but Bud continually turned and looked at June. She noticed it out of the corner of her eye, and it thrilled her. They slowed down as they came to the road going to White Eagle.

"Perhaps it would be better if you went the rest of the way alone," suggested Bud. "I don't want to cause any trouble for you—and someone might see us and tell your father."

June nodded slowly. "Yes, perhaps it would be best for now," she said.

"I hope you can remember this old trail," smiled Bud.

"Oh, I've never forgotten it," laughed June. "I haven't been on it for a long time."

"Thanks so much, Junie," said Bud, holding out his hand to her.

She took his hand and squeezed it tightly.

"Until next time," said June as she swung her horse up the hill in front of them.

Bud sat there and watched her disappear into the brush above him. Then he swung his horse around and rode slowly down the road to Moolock.

Frank Allenby met Ed Clayton in town and together they spoke to Dr. Edwell regarding the condition of Jim Seeley.

"He's still unconscious and, in my opinion, he hasn't a chance," said the old doctor, wiping his bald head with his handkerchief.

"Is there any chance he'll regain consciousness?" asked Allenby.

"I doubt it very much," replied Doc Edwell.

"If he could only come to long enough to tell us who shot him," said Clayton.

"I'll watch him closely," said Doc. "If he gains consciousness, I'll see what I can get from him, but I doubt if he ever will."

Allenby and Clayton left the doctor's house, climbed in the buggy, and headed for the Half-Circle Cross ranch. Allenby was in a vile mood as he drove the team at top speed over the rough dirt road. Ed Clayton held onto the seat with one hand and his hat with the other.

The buggy swung into the ranch yard and up to the front porch in a cloud of dust. Clayton looked at Allenby when he stopped the team, but he knew better than to say anything.

"I'm going to get to the bottom of things," snorted Allenby as he climbed out of the buggy and tied the reins to a porch post. "I've had it—that's all!"

"What are you going to do?" asked Clayton as

he got out and shook himself all over.

"Follow me," Frank said as he headed for the bunkhouse.

Two saddle horses were standing at the stable, so he knew Chet Hobson and Omaha Olsen were back. They went into the bunkhouse.

Harry Allenby was sober but a bit shaky as he squinted at his father and Clayton. Hobson was sitting at the table in the center of the room, cleaning his gun. Omaha was sprawled on his bunk. They all looked at the newcomers.

"It's time we got things straight around here," said Frank Allenby. "I hired Jim Seeley on advice from Ed Clayton. Seeley is a private detective. He was working for me when he was shot down."

Allenby paused and looked from one to the other. Omaha was amused, but Hobson was serious as he looked up at the rancher. Harry seemed indifferent to it all.

"Someone shot Seeley down like a dog," Frank continued. "They probably have added murder to their other crimes. There is no doubt in my mind that either the sheriff and his deputy, or one of those two strange cowboys turned that pinto and gray horse loose, to ruin the evidence.

"Just what interest those two cowboys have in this deal, I do not know. I feel sure that Swan River Smith thought those two horses were in his stable, and that he was as surprised as anyone when we didn't find them. The sheriff is against us; so it is up to us to handle it in the only way possible—go and settle it ourselves."

"How do you mean?" asked Hobson.

"I mean that we'll ride down to the HB ranch, force them to confess, and take them to jail ourselves," said Allenby.

"Christmas daisies!" grunted Omaha. "You talk like we was going out to bring in a cow."

Allenby glared at Omaha. He did not believe in anyone questioning an order or suggestion from him.

"Are you afraid to do this, Omaha?" he asked.

"No, I ain't afraid," said Omaha. "I just don't think it can be done, that's all. You might get a hell of a lot of hot lead, but you won't get no confession."

"Would you refuse to go?" asked Allenby.

Omaha looked up at the ceiling for several moments before he looked at Allenby and nodded slowly.

"Yeah, I reckon I would. If I caught a man stealing your cows, I'd shoot him as quick as you would. But I don't reckon I'm going to try and take the law in my own hands and try to make a man confess. That's up to the law officers—not me."

"All right," said Allenby, straightening to his full height. "Your wages up to date are ready for you, Olsen. I want men who will do my bidding. How about you, Hobson?"

"I'll ride with Omaha," said Hobson calmly. "We came here together, you know. I've handled your cows, Allenby. You handle your own killings."

Allenby snorted and looked around. He had been sure of Hobson because Hobson was his foreman. It only left three to do the job—and he wasn't so sure of Ed Clayton.

"Well, that makes things different," he decided grudgingly.

"Decidedly," agreed Clayton. "Perhaps the idea wasn't as good as it might have been. You see, Allenby, you haven't enough evidence yet to force a confession from either of the Bell family."

"Well, how can I get it?" demanded Allenby. "I'd give five thousand dollars for evidence enough to convict those two men."

No one seemed to know, which was not surprising.

"Who are those two strange cowboys?" asked Allenby.

"One is named Slade and the other one's O'Day," said Harry. "I heard that much about them. The tall one is called Silent."

Allenby squinted closely at Harry.

"Are you sure of that, Harry?" he asked.

"Well, that's what they're called."

"That's funny," muttered Allenby, turning to Clayton. "Those are the names of the two men that Freeman, the secretary of the Cattle Association, spoke to me about. They refused my offer, but still they came here."

"Slade and O'Day, eh?" said Clayton wonderingly. "Who sent them here, I wonder?"

"I've done a lot of wondering and I'm through," declared Allenby, turning to the door. "I'm going to town and find those two men. My offer is still open, and I think they'll accept it after I tell them what it means to me."

"How soon can I get my pay?" asked Omaha.

Allenby halted halfway outside and looked back.

"Meet me in town and we'll take care of it. Are you going with me, Clayton?"

"Yes, I'll go with you," agreed Clayton.

They went up to the house, but did not go inside. They climbed into the buggy with Allenby driving and headed back toward Moolock.

Omaha sat up on his bunk, a broad grin on his face as he looked at Hobson.

"I suppose that me and you are canned, Chet," he said.

"You're canned," corrected Hobson. "I quit."

"Aw, hell!" blurted Harry. "The old man will forget all that in an hour. You fellows got anything drinkable around here?"

"You lay off the booze," advised Hobson. "The first thing you'll know, the old man will cut you out of his will."

"Is that so?" Harry laughed sarcastically. "That'll hurt me a hell of a lot. He never did give me a rotten cent; and he'll live longer than I will probably."

"If you don't keep your mouth shut," Hobson agreed dryly.

Harry laughed and got to his feet. "I don't want to see you fellows leave," he said.

Hobson glanced at him. "Would you have ridden into the HB with your father and Clayton to get the Bells to confess?"

"Well, hell, no!" Harry snapped. "Dad gets hot-headed and doesn't think at times."

"It seems to run in the family," Omaha remarked as he pulled his war sack out from under the bunk.

"Aw, think it over," pleaded Harry. "I can't run this place alone."

"Maybe your father will help you," Hobson chuckled as he secured his war sack.

Harry grunted, turned, and left the bunkhouse. Omaha and Hobson laughed as they quickly packed their war sacks. When they came out of the bunkhouse, June Allenby came riding into the yard and up to the stable. She stopped next to their two horses. She dismounted and looked closely at them.

"Where are you going?" she asked curiously.

"I'm fired—and Chet quit," grinned Omaha.

"Who did that?"

"Your father," replied Hobson as he fastened his war sack on the back of his saddle. "We refused to be part of his raiding party on the HB ranch."

June sighed. "I'm sorry," she said.

"You don't have to be," grinned Omaha. "We liked it here, but when Chet and me took the job ten years ago, we figured it was just temporary."

They all laughed, and June shook hands with both men; then she went up to the ranch house.

"One good Allenby," sighed Omaha.

"Two," corrected Hobson. "You forget Mrs. Allenby."

They mounted their horses and rode slowly out of the ranch yard while Harry, June, and Mrs. Allenby stood by windows in the front room and watched them leave.

"Now what are we going to do?" asked Mrs. Allenby.

"Let Pa worry about it. It was his fault," grunted Harry. "He never can be content to let things be."

Dr. Edwell was standing on the walk in front of the Elk Saloon with Swan River Smith when Frank Allenby and Clayton drove into town. The doctor motioned for the men to pull over to the walk.

"What's the matter," asked Allenby, sensing something was wrong.

"Seeley died about half an hour ago," replied Doc.

"Well," sighed Allenby. "We did expect it."

"Do you know where he came from?" asked Doc.

Allenby shook his head and looked at Clayton.

"Ed, do you know? You sent for him."

"I only knew that he was in Omaha, but I know nothing more about him or his family," replied Clayton. "Too bad."

"Yes, it is," nodded Swan River. "We don't know what to do with the body."

"You'll have to bury him here," said Allenby. "I'll pay whatever the expenses are, since he was working for me."

"That's mighty fine of you, Mr. Allenby," nodded Doc Edwell. "I'll take care of the arrangements."

Allenby and Clayton tied up the buggy and went into the Elk Saloon while Swan River crossed the street to his office where Forty Dollar, Silent, and Irish were seated around the desk with Silent doing some card tricks for them. They looked up at the sheriff as he entered.

"Seeley died a while ago," said Swan River as he tossed his hat on a cot and sank down in his chair behind the desk, squinting at the card layout on his desk top. "Never regained consciousness."

"Too bad." Silent shook his head sadly. "Did you find out anything more about him?"

"Allenby hired him; he was a detective," replied the sheriff. "That's what I know."

Silent said, "It kind of looks to me like his profession reacted upon him. Someone must have learned who he was."

"Perhaps," grunted Swan River. "That's why Allenby told me to keep out of it—he was going to do it his way."

"Where'd he get Seeley?"

"Ed Clayton recommended him to Allenby," replied Swan River. "He knew him from some previous work they had done together. Or somesuch."

"What are they going to do with the body?" asked Forty Dollar.

"Bury it," replied Swan River. "What did you think they were going to do with it, stuff it?"

Silent reached out and pulled all the cards to himself; then he quickly stacked them. Everyone was silent, watching him as he shuffled the deck with one hand and spread out the cards, face up.

"All kinds of cards in this deck," said Silent slowly as he looked at the sheriff across the desk. "Just like all kinds of people—and perhaps one or two are the ones you want for the problems they have caused around here. You can pick a card easily, but you can't pick out the person or persons you need."

Swan River grunted, but nodded his head.

"I wished I could pick out the person who killed Seeley," he said.

"What about the train robbers, and the rustlers who took Allenby's cows out of the corrals?" queried Forty Dollar.

"There you go, adding coals to the fire," groaned Swan River.

"I never added nothing," snorted Forty Dollar. "They've always been right there."

Silent grinned and held the cards out to the deputy, who looked at them.

"You pick out a card, Forty Dollar," said Silent.

The deputy studied the cards, then picked the three of spades. "That looks like the dirty villian," he grinned.

Silent stacked the rest of the cards, shuffled them several times, then put the deck on the top of the desk.

"Put your treasured card into the deck, anywhere."

Forty Dollar squinted at his card, then at the deck. Finally, he shoved the card into the upper part of the deck and looked at Silent, who had taken out his knife and opened the large blade.

"Whatcha going to do?" Forty gasped, pulling his hand back quickly.

"Just watch," replied Silent as he picked up the deck and worked the edges a little.

Then, with the deck in his left hand, he picked up the knife in his right hand and got to his feet. While everyone watched him, Silent moved around the desk and stopped, looking at the blank wall next to the door leading back to the jail.

"Mind if I use your wall here, Swan River?" he asked.

"Use my wall?" parroted the sheriff. "Go ahead."

With a quick flip of his left wrist, Silent sent the cards spinning against the wall, and at the same time his right hand flipped his knife at the wall. All but one card fell to the floor. That card was pinned face against the wall.

"Forty Dollar, fetch that card, will you?" asked Silent.

The deputy grunted as he got to his feet and stepped over and pulled the knife out of the wall and took the playing card off the sharp blade. He looked at the card, then quickly at Silent.

"My three of spades!" he exclaimed, holding the card up for the others to see. "Silent, how did you do such a thing?"

"Magic," laughed the tall cowboy as he took his knife from the deputy, closed it, and put it in his pocket.

"Didja see that, Swan River—didja?" gasped the deputy.

"Of course, I saw it—but I don't believe it."

"That's the way things go," said Silent as he sat down again at the desk. "The guilty ones will be caught, Sheriff."

"I sure hope so," sighed Swan River. "Murder is murder, by golly! That Seeley was shot from behind, and it ain't no ways healthy nor conductive of pleasant thoughts to think that there might be a killer behind the next bush."

"Looks to me like it might be a warning," grunted Forty Dollar. "I sure believe in them kind of signs. I've had my fortune told five times altogether, by five different persons—and each one was different. I don't know which one to believe."

"I never had my fortune told," said Swan River. "I'd a lot rather get along in my own dumb way. I don't want to know what's just around the next corner; but I'd sure like to have just a little inside information on who's doing this dirty work."

"Maybe Seeley had inside information," suggested Silent. "Something led him into the shooting."

"Oh, shucks," the sheriff grunted. "Inquest tomorrow morning. I hate them. Never get much information and they pile everything on the sheriff's shoulders."

Just then Doc Edwell came through the open doorway. He stopped at the desk next to the sheriff, talking jerkily.

"Very little information to be had," he declared. "Seeley came here from Omaha, Nebraska. Pockets yielded very little. Nothing worthwhile. Here." He handed the sheriff a soiled envelope. "That is a letter to Seeley, written, I presume, by Ed Clayton. I've read it."

Swan River took the letter out of the envelope and read it carefully. Swan River did not read very fast. Finally, he placed it on his desk.

"Well, that don't give us much information, Doc," he said. "We'll just have to go ahead and hold the inquest in the morning, bring in the usual verdict, and bury the corpse, I reckon."

"Yes, yes, I suppose so, Sheriff. Well, good-bye, gentlemen."

The doctor bustled away, as busy as a bee. Silent picked up the letter and looked at it. It had been sent from Moolock, and was directed to Jim Seeley, Omaha, Nebraska, care of General Delivery. The letter read:

Dear Jim:

Frank Allenby, the biggest cattleman in Moolock, is up against a very dangerous proposition and needs help. It looks like a plain case of spite work by somebody and you can make five thousand dollars for a few days' work. This gang of rustlers are able to pull off big jobs and get away without the slightest chance of anyone detecting them. Your work must be done without anyone knowing who you are, *sabe?*

I will explain everything to you when you get here. You will like Allenby. If you can't take this job, Jim, it will disappoint me greatly. If you come, keep it dark or it might make things very bad. Wire your decision.

Sincerely,
Ed

"Well, Allenby's life is still worth the five thousand, I reckon," smiled Silent as he handed the letter back to the sheriff. "Maybe he'll raise the ante after a while."

"He'll never raise it!" snorted Swan River.

Irish said, "I've heard of horses that sold for that much."

"A horse worth five thousand?" gasped Forty Dollar.

"Some are," nodded Irish. "We seen them in Frisco. They use them for some kind of a game. What was that game, Silent?"

"Polo," replied Silent. "Yes, some horseflesh is worth a lot more than Allenby."

"Speak about the devil," muttered Forty Dollar.

They all turned to see Frank Allenby entering the office, but he didn't hear what had been said. Allenby was trying his best to be pleasant as he greeted all of them. He sat down in an empty chair and fanned himself with his hat.

"Going to hold the inquest tomorrow?" he asked the sheriff.

"Yeah, tomorrow morning," nodded Swan River. "Probably want you to testify, Allenby. It won't amount to anything; but it's according to law."

"Certainly," agreed Allenby warmly. "I wish I could give you more information regarding this man Seeley; but I know nothing about him. There is no question but that he was murdered."

"Well," said Swan River slowly, "I never knowed a man to shoot himself twice in the back with a rifle. So I reckon we've got to look the facts square in the face and admit that Seeley was shot with malice aforethought and a high-powered rifle."

"Mmm," muttered Allenby.

Swan River's face was so serious that Allenby wasn't quite sure whether Swan River was joking or not. He decided to drop the subject; so he turned to Silent and said:

"I was just wondering if you two cowboys were looking for work."

Silent grinned widely. "You might change that question to read, looking for jobs, and get us to nod our heads."

Allenby forced a laugh. "I suppose it's just as well to be honest about it," he said. "There will probably be two vacancies on my ranch, and you two can have the jobs, if you care to take them."

"Hobson and Omaha quitting?" asked Forty Dollar.

"Well, it amounts to that. I shall make Harry my foreman, I think. He needs responsibilities."

"He sure as blazes needs something," grinned Swan River.

Allenby's lips formed a hot retort, but he curbed his feelings. He knew that there was nothing to gain in quarreling with the sheriff, so he shut his lips and waited for Silent to decide.

"Forty a month?" asked Irish.

"Yes."

The forty dollars per month did not appeal to Irish, but he was willing to leave the decision to Silent, who was thinking deeply over the offer.

"Well," Silent said slowly. "I suppose we might take it. It ain't none of our business, but I'd like to know why your foreman and the other man are quitting you."

Allenby's expression indicated that indeed it was none of Silent's business, but he replied evenly:

"They are leaving the Half-Circle Cross because they would not obey my orders."

"Yeah? Well, maybe we won't obey them either, Allenby. But if you want to take that chance, we're willing, eh, Irish?"

"We can always quit," said Irish indifferently.

"Well, that is settled," said Allenby with a certain amount of satisfaction as he started for the door. "You will be out to the ranch today?"

"Before suppertime," said Silent.

A few minutes later, Silent, from the sheriff's office door, saw Omaha Olsen and Chet Hobson ride into town with their war sacks tied to the back of their saddles. Allenby met them in front of the Elk Saloon and paid what was due on their salaries.

Silent watched Allenby climb into his buggy and start out of town. He turned and looked at Irish, who shook his head.

"What did you take these jobs for?" Irish asked.

"Our pocketbook is low, pardner," grinned Silent. "We'll test it out and see what it's like."

They went to the hotel, paid their bill, picked up their belongings, and went to the stable where they saddled their horses and rode out of town, heading for the Half-Circle Cross ranch.

"We really didn't need this job," said Irish as they rode along.

"Just a foolish notion, that's all," grunted Silent.

"All right," Irish said grudgingly. "Forty a month, and take orders from some kid."

"We ain't took no orders from him yet, Irish."

"That's true. I'd kind of like to know what kind of orders Allenby passed out to them other two hired men."

"Wait and see," advised Silent. "We'll likely find out."

About two miles out of town they overtook Frank Allenby, who had driven off to the side of the road in the shade of a large oak and was waiting for them.

"I didn't want to say too much there in town," he said to them. "Freeman told me your names at the time he spoke about me hiring you; so I know you are the same men. I think I need your help now more than I did before, and I just want to say that I'm still willing to pay you the sum of five thousand dollars for evidence that will convict those who have been stealing my stock.

"The men who have been stealing my stock are the same ones that killed Seeley. A conviction for rustling will fasten the murder on them also. I'm particularly interested in nailing Bud Bell. For some reason or other, it appears that we have been working at cross-purposes. I think you know what I mean."

"Don't reckon I do," said Silent thoughtfully.

"That matter concerning the pinto and gray horses."

"Oh, yeah. I heard the sheriff saying something about it. What was it all about, Allenby?"

Allenby studied Silent and Irish for several moments. Irish's expression was as innocent as that of a child, while Silent's was merely indifferent.

"Well," said Allenby dubiously. "Perhaps—but it doesn't matter."

He spoke sharply to the team, which surged back into the road, and the two cowboys followed leisurely behind him.

CHAPTER SIX

Frank Allenby and his son Harry left the Half-Circle Cross ranch right after breakfast so they could attend the inquest. Allenby told Silent and Irish to look over the ranch and get acquainted with it, so the two men spent some time looking the place over.

"This ranch has been well taken care of," remarked Irish.

"It sure is kind of dudelike," admitted Silent. "But you have to excuse Allenby; he's from the city. If he runs cows long enough, he'll develop squeaky hinges, bare floors, and weather-beaten exteriors."

"Makes me feel like I'm civilized," grunted Irish as they stopped by the corrals next to the stable. "Even the bunkhouse door doesn't squeak. By golly,

I'd put some sand into them hinges if I stayed here long. Carpet on the bunkhouse floor and a big can for cigarette butts!"

Silent chuckled. "First class, pardner."

"I'd rather go third class," sighed Irish as he climbed up on the fence and sat down on the top pole.

"Suit yourself," said Silent. "I'm going to get better acquainted with the Chinese cook."

"That's a good idea," laughed Irish as he watched the tall cowboy saunter up to the kitchen door.

He opened it and went inside. Meanwhile, Irish took a deep breath and began to whistle.

Wham! A bullet went past Irish's head and embedded itself in the side of the stable. Zing! This bullet came closer as Irish struggled to free his trousers from a nail in the corral fence. The third bullet found its mark, and Irish went head over heels off the fence and huddled on the ground.

From the kitchen door Silent came on the run, gun in hand, followed by the Chinese cook and June Allenby.

"Get down!" yelled Silent as he skidded to his knees beside Irish.

Zing! Another bullet whined off the gravel near Silent, causing him to roll away from Irish and in against the corral fence. Silent got to his knees, peering through the fence, trying to find out where the shooting was coming from.

"See anything?" asked June.

Silent turned and saw June and the cook huddled beside a large tree trunk. He turned and searched the hillside at the rear of the ranch, but he saw nothing. He waited a while, but there was no more shooting, so he carefully crawled over to where Irish was sprawled out. He carefully turned him over.

Irish blinked up at Silent, trying to clear his head.

"I—I didn't think I was that bad a whistler," he said hoarsely.

"Where'd you get hit?"

"I think it's in my left shoulder," said Irish, trying to use his left arm, but it hurt him. "Yeah, that's where it is."

By now, June and the cook were beside Silent as he helped Irish to his feet.

"You hit?" asked the Chinese cook, looking at the blood on Irish's shirt.

"Got him in the shoulder," said Silent. "Let's get him into the house and take a good look."

"I got plenty hot wateh," said the cook as they moved toward the kitchen door.

"Who would do such a thing?" asked June, opening the door for them to go into the house.

"I wished I knew," grunted Irish.

Mrs. Allenby was standing there, nervously twisting a handkerchief in her two hands.

"Take him in the parlor," she ordered, leading the way into the plush room where she pointed to a large sofa.

Silent eased Irish down on the sofa, but he sat up.

"Doggone it," he grunted. "I want to sit up. I'm not hurt that bad."

Silent opened his shirt and took it off, exposing a bad crease where the bullet had traveled across the top of his left arm just below the shoulder point. It was bleeding.

The cook brought in a kettle of hot water and

June came into the room with some towels and bandages. Silent quickly cleaned the wound while Irish gritted his teeth with the pain of the hot water on his flesh.

"Damn poor shot," grunted Irish as he looked at the wound.

"I'm glad he was," smiled June.

"This is some way to start your first day at the ranch," said Mrs. Allenby. "We never had anyone shot here before."

"There's always a first time," grunted Irish. "Now that the first time is over, it could happen any time."

Silent worked on the wound some more, then bandaged it.

"I think you better see the doctor," he said. "He might have something that would help heal it."

"And kill me with pain," grunted Irish.

"Doc Edwell isn't that bad," said June. "In fact, he has had a fine medical education. No, he won't hurt you."

"Maybe you'll go in my place," suggested Irish, and they all laughed.

"Think you can ride?" asked Silent.

"Of course, I can ride," snorted Irish. "That bullet didn't hit me in the—pardon me, ladies."

June and Mrs. Allenby laughed as Irish got unsteadily to his feet.

"You get fixed good," said the cook. "Come back soon. I have nice apple pie ready."

"I'll be back," grinned Irish as Silent helped him out of the house. As soon as they were down at the stable alone, Irish looked sharply at his partner.

"Why did someone shoot me?" he asked.

"That's a good question, cowboy. Wished I knew the answer."

"Do you suppose someone knows why we're out here?"

"I doubt it," replied Silent. "We've just hired on as cowpunchers."

"Maybe they shoot cowpunchers out here," said Irish as he felt of his shoulder. "Feels hot."

"I'll saddle the horses," said Silent. "You wait here."

"Uh-huh," nodded Irish. "Man, that June, she's a beauty—ain't she?"

"Your rope's dragging," cautioned Silent from the stall. "I believe she's already spoken for."

"Yeah, I know. I heard she's going to marry Ed Clayton."

"That's so, eh? Never heard that."

Silent brought the two horses out and he assisted Irish into the saddle. Then they rode toward town.

"Let's be careful," suggested Silent. "We'll cut off to the left and stay off the road. There's too many places suitable for bushwhacking."

They rode across the flat ground, cut around a dry creek, and made their way into Moolock.

They rode up to the doctor's house just as the doctor and Swan River Smith were coming down the walk. They looked sharply at the two riders and noticed Irish's bandaged shoulder.

"What happened?" asked Doc Edwell.

"Got shot," replied Irish as he waited until Silent dismounted and came around to help him down.

"Who shot you?" demanded Swan River.

"Who shot Seeley?" countered Silent as they started toward the doctor's house.

Swan River squinted sideways at Silent as they went up the porch.

"I'll take care of this, gents," said Doc as he led Irish into the house.

"All right, what happened?" asked the sheriff as he and Silent sat down on the porch railing to wait.

Silent told what he knew of the shooting.

The sheriff listened intently, shaking his head. "Why in blazes would they shoot Irish?"

"Maybe they didn't like his whistling," grinned Silent.

"Aw, that's no reason."

"Have you ever heard him, Swan River?"

"That bad, huh?" Swan River shook his head. "Reckon his whistle sure must carry to reach someone back in the hills."

"How was the inquest?" asked Silent, changing the subject.

"How is any inquest?" grunted the sheriff. "Same old thing. Could have told you before it happened. Waste of time, I'd say."

"How was Frank Allenby?"

"In his glory," snorted Swan River. "That fool milked the inquest. You'd think he was one of them stage people trying to act."

"I figured he'd enjoy every minute of it," sighed Silent. "Even at the expense of a dead man."

"Forty Dollar is down at the office making a list of the crimes we've got to solve—and now I've got another to add to it," sighed the sheriff. "Too bad you or Irish didn't see who was behind that rifle."

"If I'd a-seen him, you'd have another body to take care of," said Silent. "This country is really salty."

"Hate," snorted Swan River. "I told you, there's hate all over this valley."

"That covers a lot of territory," said Silent as the door opened and Irish came out with Doc Edwell.

"I'm afraid he'll live," Doc said, wiping his bald head with his handkerchief.

"Yeah, I'm all right—until the next bullet," grinned Irish.

"I hope there won't be another one," said Doc. "You got off mighty lucky with this one. A little space over and you'd be through for good."

"I'll remember that, Doc, and stand sideways all the time," laughed Irish. "Thanks for fixing me up."

"Your pardner did a good job. Wasn't much for me to do. Better come in day after tomorrow or thereabouts and let me look at it," said Doc as he turned and went back into the house.

The three men walked out to the horses. Silent and Irish mounted while Swan River started on foot down the street.

"I think I could stand a drink," said Irish.

Silent nodded as they rode down to the Elk Saloon and tied up their horses. As they went up to the doorway, they met Frank Allenby and Harry coming out.

Frank stopped short, squinting at them. "What are you two doing in here?" he demanded.

"Irish was shot this morning at the ranch," explained Silent. "Had to get him to a doctor."

"Shot?" queried the older Allenby as he stepped close to Irish and looked at his bandaged shoulder. "How bad?"

"Not bad, but painful," replied Irish. "I think I could stand a drink."

"Why, of course. C'mon, we'll all have another," said Frank Allenby.

They went to the bar where they found Joe Bass, Jack Merton, and Pete Sepulveda, who all wanted to know what had happened to Irish. He told them what he knew.

"This country is going to hell," grunted Bass.

"Why would anyone shoot you, O'Day?" asked Merton.

Irish shook his head. "I wished I knew."

After a drink, Silent and Irish pulled out. Frank Allenby followed them out on the walk while Harry stayed with the men at the bar.

"Take it easy," said Allenby. "Go back to the ranch and rest. Slade, I want to have a talk with you this evening."

"I'll be there," nodded Silent as they went to their horses.

After supper, Irish went to the bunkhouse to rest while Silent went with Frank Allenby to the front porch of the house. Allenby lighted an old pipe and sat in a swing, gently moving back and forth. Silent sat on the porch railing, studying the big man.

"Who knew you were detectives?" asked Allenby.

"Detectives?" queried Silent. "We're not detectives. We're two nosey cowboys making a living."

Allenby chuckled, shaking his head.

"I know better—and you know better—and someone else knows it, too. That's why O'Day was shot today," he said, puffing on his pipe.

"Perhaps," grunted Silent.

"No perhaps, Slade," said the rancher. "They killed Seeley and now they're after you two."

"Who could they be?"

"The Bells, who else?" grunted Allenby, taking the pipe from his mouth. "They've been the cause of all my trouble. It's intensified since the young Bell returned. Oh, I know I'm right."

"But what evidence do you have?" asked Silent.

"Like that sheriff—evidence! Bah! I'll prove it—you just watch me," grunted Allenby. "I'll catch them red-handed."

"And maybe receive some hot lead for your efforts," said Silent.

"I'll take that chance!" snapped the rancher as he put the pipe back in his mouth and began puffing heavily on it. "Yes, if I have to, I'll do it alone."

"That's a big task for one man not trained to do that type of work," said Silent.

Allenby nodded. "I know, but I'm real tired of being robbed," he snorted. "Besides, you ought to think about your partner getting shot; don't you want to catch the person responsible for it?"

"I certainly do," replied Silent as he looked into Allenby's eyes, causing the big man to shift his glance away from Silent. "I'll get the person who fired that shot."

"What method will you use?"

"Method?" queried Silent, a slight smile on his lips. "Allenby, I don't use any set method. I look for proof. And I play hunches, and then sometimes I use magic."

"Magic? What tommyrot is that?"

Silent smiled as he threw his voice behind Allenby.

"You think this is tommyrot, do you?"

Allenby whirled on the swing, almost upsetting the thing and dropping his pipe into his lap. He grabbed the pipe and quickly brushed off his trousers. Then he looked behind him again, but no one was there, only the blank wall.

"What in blazes was that?" he demanded, knocking the ashes out of his pipe onto the floor.

"Magic," chuckled Silent.

"It was, eh? I don't believe it."

"You should believe it," said the voice once again.

Allenby was watching Silent closely but could not detect a movement of his lips. He shook his head.

"That's good, Slade, but what can it do to trap rustlers?"

"Who knows?" grunted Silent. "You never know what will work until the time presents itself."

"All right," Allenby said. "I see your point, Slade. I hope your magic will help me get this settled so we can live peacefully here."

Silent got to his feet and stretched.

"Think I'll check on Irish," he said as he turned and left the porch.

Allenby watched him until he went into the bunkhouse.

Irish was stretched out on his bunk, his pillow arranged so that it propped up his wounded shoulder.

He looked at Silent and grinned. "What's the bad word?" he asked.

"Nothing bad," laughed Silent as he sat down and pulled off his boots. "The old man has ideas regarding the Bell family, especially Bud, but he really has nothing to back them up. Hatred is a terrible thing, Irish."

"Yeah, I reckon it makes a person think and see things that really don't exist. He didn't give

you any orders that we wouldn't follow out, did
he?"

Silent laughed and shook his head. "Nope. He
was fairly reasonable except when he spoke of the
Bells. I think I've got him straightened out a
little—at least, I hope so."

Silent also hoped there was a good explanation
for the pinto and gray—the Bell horses—he and
Irish had inherited that night in Tecoma.

CHAPTER SEVEN

After a restless night, Irish O'Day was up before dawn and out on the corral fence, watching the first light of day come over the hills.

He gingerly felt his shoulder. It pained him, but not too badly. Just plumb annoying, he thought.

It was nearly an hour later that the Chinese cook came into the kitchen and started his work. He peered out the rear door at Irish and called to him.

"You all right?"

"Sure," replied Irish. "Couldn't sleep well, so I thought I'd get out and breathe some fresh air."

"Fresh coffee soon," the cook said as he turned back into the kitchen.

Irish grinned as he slipped down from the corral fence and sauntered up to the house. He could hear the cook humming to himself as he banged cooking utensils around. Irish opened the screen door and stepped into the room.

"Pretty soon," said the Chinese cook with a big smile. "You sit down—rest."

Irish nodded as he pulled out a chair from the long table and sat down. A sound in the doorway caused him to turn to see June Allenby as she came into the kitchen. She smiled at Irish.

"Up early, aren't you?" she asked.

Irish nodded. "What about you?"

"I awoke and decided to get up for a change," she replied as she sniffed the coffee. She pulled out a chair across the table from Irish and sat down.

"How's the shoulder?"

"It's there—and sore," replied Irish, working his left arm a little. "Hurt at times during the night, but it'll be all right."

"You'll have to be careful for a few days," said June.

"Aw," grinned Irish, "it'll be just fine."

The Chinese cook came up with two steaming cups of coffee and placed them in front of June and Irish.

"That smells mighty good, Cookie," said June.

"Help wake you up," grinned Cookie as he shuffled back to the large wood stove.

"Cookie, eh?" Irish said.

June nodded. "I don't know his real name, but we've called him Cookie ever since Pa bought the ranch. I believe Mr. Winter also called him that."

"Good a name as any," chuckled Irish as he tested the hot coffee. He shook his head and slowly blew on the scalding liquid.

"What do you think of the Half-Circle Cross?" asked June.

"It's all right," replied Irish as he sipped the drink. "But I'm used to a more run-down place."

The back door opened and Silent Slade peered inside; then his lean face broke into a wide grin.

"Thought you'd rode off," he said, coming into the room.

"Couldn't sleep, so I got up," explained Irish. "Join us for coffee."

"I'll just do that," said Silent, sitting down next to Irish.

Cookie quickly brought him a steaming cup of coffee.

"Thanks," muttered Silent.

"You all right?" queried Cookie.

"Why, certainly—why?"

"You thank me. Most cowboys never thank Cookie."

"They should," said Silent seriously. "You're the one that supplies us with food so we can work."

Cookie nodded, his face beaming. Then he turned and went back to his stove and began clattering pots and pans, humming to himself.

"You've made his day," smiled June.

Frank Allenby came into the kitchen, his shirt unbuttoned, his feet in slippers. He stopped and looked at the gathering at the table.

"Early birds," he muttered as he joined them, and Cookie brought him some coffee.

Allenby turned to Irish. "How are you doing, O'Day?"

"I could be better, but I'm all right," replied Irish with a grin. "There was pain during the night, and I couldn't get comfortable. But now that I'm up, it feels a lot better."

"That's good," grunted the rancher, sipping his coffee. "There's not too much to do around the

ranch." He paused and looked at Silent. "Harry
and I must go into town this morning. You can
ride in or stay here and check the livestock."

"I'll check things," said Silent. "Perhaps this
afternoon Irish and I can ride back into the hills
and look around."

"Good idea," said Allenby. "Where's Harry?"

"Asleep," said Irish. "He didn't get home very
early."

"Drinking again?" queried Allenby.

"I don't know," replied Irish. "I was awake, but
he was very quiet."

Allenby nodded as he pushed back from the table and walked to the rear door.

"I'll wake him," he said as he strode out of the
house.

June looked sharply at Irish. "Was he drunk?"
she asked.

Irish started to shrug his shoulder, forgetting
his wound Then he grimaced and shook his head.

"I really don't know," he said.

"Thank you," sighed June. "He's had this terrible habit ever since we came here from Philadelphia."

"It's hard on a young man once he starts," said
Silent.

"Bleakfast ready," called Cookie. "You get big
boss."

"He'll be back in a few minutes," said June. "We
can go ahead and eat, Cookie."

Frank Allenby returned when they were about
finished. Harry was dragging along behind him,
his face an ashen color, his eyes bloodshot. They
sat down and Cookie served them their breakfast.
Frank Allenby ate heartily, but Harry merely

played with the food, set the fork down, and shook his head.

"Not hungry?" asked Irish.

Harry shook his head, got to his feet, and walked to the doorway. There he stopped and looked back at the group.

"I'll get our horses ready, Pa," he said, then disappeared.

Allenby's face showed displeasure as he ate in silence. Silent and Irish excused themselves and left the kitchen.

June looked intently at her father.

"Stop staring at me like I'm a freak!" he snorted.

"You made Harry that way, Pa," accused June. "He was a decent young man when we came out here."

"I had nothing to do with him becoming a drunkard!"

"Yes, you did!" snapped June, getting to her feet. "You didn't show him any consideration. In fact, you never show any to Mother or me."

Allenby banged a fist on the table, causing the plates to wobble.

"I don't have to take that from you!" he snapped, getting to his feet and facing his daughter.

"I don't blame Chet and Omaha for leaving," said June softly. "I don't see how anyone can work for you."

June whirled around and stomped out of the kitchen, leaving Frank Allenby sputtering and stammering. Cookie, his eyes wide, tried not to laugh out loud, but his body was jerking as he held it in.

Allenby turned and followed June out of the kitchen, but when he came into the parlor, she was nowhere to be seen. He shook his head, sighed deeply, and walked down the hall to his bedroom.

Silent and Irish went to the stable where Harry was struggling to saddle the two horses, so Silent stepped in and assisted him.

"You didn't have to do that," said Harry.

"I know," nodded Silent. "Why don't you try to change, Harry? Think of what you're doing to your family."

"Huh?" grunted the young man as he took the reins of the two horses and started out of the stable.

The two cowboys sat on a bench in front of the bunkhouse and watched Allenby and his son ride out of the yard and head for Moolock.

About an hour after they left, June came out of the house dressed in jeans and high-heeled riding boots. In her right hand she carried her Stetson. She came up to the two men.

"Slade, will you saddle my bronc for me?" she asked.

"Glad to," nodded Silent as he moved into the stable.

"Going for a ride?" asked Irish.

"It's nice—and the fresh air might help me a lot," she replied.

"Lots of nice places to ride around here," said Irish.

"I like to go back in the hills where I can think while I look over the valley."

Silent brought out her horse and she slipped into the saddle and, with a curt wave, rode away.

"Beautiful girl—but she's got something on her mind," said Irish.

"Living around here burdens one's mind," muttered Silent.

"I feel sorry for Mrs. Allenby," grunted Irish. "She seems to be the only sensible one around here."

"What about Cookie?" grinned Silent.

"He's a darn good cook," said Irish.

While Frank Allenby met with Ed Clayton at the hotel in Moolock, Harry headed for the Elk Saloon. The rancher and cattle-buyer sat on the hotel porch and started to talk.

"No matter how loud I yell, no one pays any attention to me," groaned Allenby.

"Perhaps if you didn't yell, but instituted some action, you might get more attention," suggested Clayton.

"You saw how far I got the other day at the ranch," snorted Allenby. "Slade doesn't think I have any evidence to move on the Bells."

"Just how good do you think Slade and O'Day are?"

"They were highly recommended by Bob Freeman of the association," replied Allenby. "I'll give them a few days. O'Day's getting shot has slowed them down some."

"That was a queer deal," grunted Clayton. "Why would anyone want to shoot him?"

"Go ahead and guess—that's what we've done," Allenby sighed, shaking his head. "We haven't an answer, but he did get shot right there at my ranch."

"Well," muttered Clayton, rubbing the back of his neck, "I don't know what this country is—"

His words stopped when someone up the street let out a wild yell. Allenby and Clayton turned to look just as the stage from White Eagle swung wildly around the corner and into the main street,

with the driver, Shorty Elkins, sitting straight in
the seat, hanging on with both hands, and with
the lines twisted around one foot and held between
his knees.

The team went past the stage station, catching
the right front wheel at the post of the hitchrack
and jerking to a sudden stop, so sudden that Shorty
fell over the wheel and hit the boardwalk, where
he stayed.

Allenby and Clayton got to their feet and hurried over. A crowd was gathering. Swan River
Smith and Forty Dollar came running across the
street from the sheriff's office.

They straightened Shorty Elkins out on the walk
and someone poured a drink of whisky between
his white lips.

"My gosh!" exploded Larry Neil, an Arrowhead
cowboy. "Someone has sure riddled poor Shorty
with bullets. Somebody get the doctor!"

Swan River knelt beside the fallen man as
Allenby and Clayton moved in behind the sheriff.
Another drink of whisky, forced between Shorty's
lips, seemed to revive him.

"How are you, Shorty?" asked Swan River. "Can
you tell us what happened to you?"

Shorty's eyes were filming, but he was conscious. He tried to lift his hand, but the effort was
too much. Several times he twisted his lips, trying
to speak. Then he said hoarsely:

"June—Allenby—"

"What about her, Shorty?" asked Swan River
eagerly. "Try it again, son."

"She—" He tried to say more, but he was unable
to open his mouth again.

"Shorty's dead," said Swan River softly, getting
to his feet.

Fred Hartwell, owner of the stage line, forced his way over and looked down at the dead man who had been his driver. Swan River told him all they knew about it, and they watched Hartwell as he examined the contents of the stage.

"The treasure box is gone," he said. "We won't know how much has been stolen until we check up with the office in White Eagle."

Doc Edwell arrived and, after a short examination, shook his head as he listened to a description of how the stage had arrived.

"I don't see how he lived that long," declared Doc. "He must have fought hard against it."

"But what about my daughter?" asked Allenby anxiously. "What could he have meant?"

"She wasn't on the stage today, was she?" asked Swan River.

"No. She was at the ranch when I left there." Allenby whirled and pushed through the crowd to the hitchrack at the Elk Saloon where he mounted quickly and headed out of town.

"Some of us better ride to the Half-Circle Cross," said the sheriff quickly. "Shorty had that girl on his mind for some reason. Dang it! Too bad he didn't live longer."

Swan River and Forty made their way swiftly toward their stable behind the sheriff's office. Several cowboys mounted and waited for the law officers to ride with them. Ed Clayton had gotten a horse and was following Allenby to the ranch.

Silent and Irish were in the bunkhouse when the cavalcade arrived. Allenby and Clayton were not trained horsemen, and they were soon overtaken by the sheriff and his men. Silent peered

out the window and saw the riders, so he and Irish
hurried outside.

Allenby fairly fell out of his saddle, staggering
to catch his balance. Silent grabbed him to keep
him from going down.

"Is June home?" the rancher panted.

Silent shook his head.

"No, she ain't. She left a while after you did this
morning. She had me saddle her horse and she
rode away. I don't reckon she's come back yet.
What's the matter?"

Allenby groaned and headed for the house.

"What's the matter?" Silent repeated as he
looked at the sheriff.

"Stage was held up, the driver shot to ribbons.
But before he died in town, he mentioned June
Allenby. But that's all we could get out of him,"
explained Swan River. "You say, she went riding.
Which way did she go?"

"Went east from here," said Silent, pointing in
that direction.

"Straight toward the White Eagle road," said a
cowboy.

"We'll spread out and comb that country,"
snapped Swan River. "Maybe we can find her."

Mrs. Allenby met her husband on the front
porch, wondering why all the riders were at the
ranch. He quickly told her, and they held onto each
other. Tears welled up in her eyes as she looked
up at Allenby, who was also moist about the eyes.

Down by the bunkhouse, Swan River looked the
group over, and quickly divided them into two sec-
tions, putting Forty Dollar in charge of one of them.
Silent and Irish got their horses, and Irish, despite

his shoulder, saddled his horse and was determined to ride with the men.

"Two men have been murdered around here, and O'Day shot," said Swan River grimly as he looked at the men. "Be prepared for anything."

Allenby, after a few words with his wife, left and joined the men, riding with Clayton, who had been assigned to the group led by Forty Dollar. The two groups both headed east. Silent and Irish were the last ones to see June, so they headed for that spot with Swan River and his group of riders.

Both groups fanned out, searching all along the way until they reached the road to White Eagle, which ran north and south. It was here that the riders drew together, searching along the road for the spot where the stage had been held up. The road was so hard that it was impossible to distinguish anything out of the ordinary; so the searchers split into two parties again, going in opposite directions.

Silent and Irish joined Swan River Smith, going toward Moolock, and they were the ones to find the spot. It was in a timbered swale, where a small stream trickled across the road. The signs were fairly plain here. The stage had swerved half off the road into softer ground.

To the west of the road a deep cattle trail wound down the swale, where the timber would mask it from the road. Silent discovered the trail, and in it were the fresh imprints of a shod horse.

"She came down this trail," he told the sheriff, pointing out the tracks. "They picked a dandy place for the job, too. It kind of looks like she busted right into the holdup, without knowing it was taking place. She couldn't see the road until she came out through that timber, and they likely saw her first."

"Yeah," nodded Swan River. "It looks that way, Slade. Maybe they had to do something to save themselves. If it was somebody she knew—well, it kind of put them up against it."

Silent examined the tracks closely, squatting on his heels. Swan River turned around to take another look at the trail, and Silent suddenly reached down, picked up a tiny object, and put it quickly in his pocket.

"Where'll we go now?" he asked Swan River as he straightened up.

"The Lord only knows," said the bewildered sheriff. "There's no way to track them. I've heard about savages being able to follow a trail where they wasn't any, but I'm no savage. Dang it all, that's the worst part of being a sheriff. Everybody expects him to be totally wise—and with a nose like a bloodhound."

"Might as well wait for the rest of the gang to come," said Silent. "They'll be busting back this way soon. It was a cinch that Shorty Elkins didn't drive an awful long way, shot up that way."

"This is awful," grunted Irish. "Why'd they take June?"

"They took her to save their hides!" snorted Swan River.

They wandered aimlessly about, looking for some clues; but there were none. It was possibly half an hour before the other riders arrived, and Silent showed Allenby what had happened at that spot.

Allenby listened dumbly, nodding his head like a man who is too sick to talk.

"You think then that she was merely captured

to prevent her from exposing the bandits?" queried Clayton.

"That's about the only way to look at it," said Silent. "Men don't steal girls these days. It just ain't done. I don't know this country like some of you do." Silent turned to the crowd. "If any of you was going to steal a girl, where would you hide her?"

No one replied. Allenby stared dumbly ahead of him, his jaw shut tightly.

"I don't know where to look," confessed Swan River. "It's likely the same gang that held up the train."

Allenby turned quickly and stared at the sheriff. "The same two?" he asked wearily. "Why— sure!" He turned and mounted his horse.

"Where are you going?" asked Swan River.

Allenby picked up his reins, adjusted his belt. "I'm going to kill the men who own a black-headed pinto and a gray horse," he said coldly. "I'm going, if I have to go alone."

"Hank Bell," grunted Forty Dollar softly.

"Let's talk about it a little," advised Swan River. "They—"

"They wasn't in town today," interrupted Larry Neil.

"Neither were we," said Silent, indicating himself and Irish.

"They've been stealing from me for two years or more," said Allenby. "I helped to send Bud Bell to the penitentiary. Hank Bell swore he'd get even with me. Their last steal was when they took three hundred Herefords from the Moolock loading pens.

"I hired a detective and they killed him—shot him in the back. The sheriff can't deny that he thinks they robbed the train. He chased them to Tecoma, where they stole Slade's and O'Day's horses, leaving the pinto and gray in their stead. If they'd steal my cattle, rob trains—is there any reason why they wouldn't rob a stage and steal my daughter?"

"Why sit here and argue about it?" asked Harry Allenby as he moved forward. "Let's go over to the HB and have it out with them!"

"Allenby's argument looks plausible to me," stated Merton. "It's worth working on, ain't it?"

"Worth working on, but it ain't worth killing on," said Swan River. "It's awful easy to make mistakes."

"Well, I'm going down there," declared Allenby. "If I have to go alone, I'll go anyway. I'm going to find June."

"That's fine," said Silent. "We're all looking for her, Allenby, but we ain't on no killing spree. If I'm any judge of humanity, Hank, Bud, and Sticky Clay all know their shooting irons. If we go down there, hunting for trouble, I'll bet we find it. What do you think, fellows?"

"I don't care what they think!" snarled Allenby. "I'm going!"

"Wait a minute," begged Clayton. "Slade is right, Allenby. Right now you're in no frame of mind to go there. You know that those three men are dangerous. You're not a gunman. You wouldn't have one chance in a thousand with them. No, you can't get June back with a six-gun."

"You are all against me," said Allenby, a strange tone to his voice. "Don't you want me to get my little daughter back? Don't you? You're all out to get me, aren't you?"

Silent said, "This is no time for hysterics. We have to work together."

Harry moved his horse close to Silent. "You can let up on that stuff," he ordered. "You can't come in here and tell us what to do."

Silent grinned at Harry, and the boy's face flushed hotly.

"Back up, you fool!" snorted Forty Dollar. "If you don't keep your mouth shut, Harry, somebody'll hit you so hard they'll uncork you!"

Harry turned in his saddle and glared at Forty Dollar. "Look, I don't have to take things like that," he blurted.

"No, you don't have to," said Forty Dollar quietly. "If you've got any good ideas on how to handle this situation, you might step up and disgorge them. If you ain't—shut up!"

"There's a lot of truth in that," agreed Clayton.

"Oh, go to blazes!" Harry was sufficiently squelched to draw his horse back, but his face was black with rage.

The sun was just going down behind the hills, and they all knew that there was little daylight left to work in.

"If Slade is right in his surmise, I don't think that June will be injured in any way," said Clayton. "I don't think it's a situation that can be handled by force of arms. If we were lucky enough to blunder into them, it's hard to tell what they might do to keep her from exposing them to the law."

"That sounds like sense," agreed Silent heartily. "This thing is not going to be easy to handle, nor is it a mob job. I'd suggest that we go home. Maybe the girl wasn't caught at all. We kind of went off half-cocked, just because a dying man spoke her name. We don't know for sure, don't you see?"

"That's true," agreed Allenby, willing to grasp at any straw.

"I wonder if that isn't true?" said Clayton, visibly relieved.

"Let's look at it that way," suggested Swan River. "Tomorrow is another day."

After a few minutes of conversation, Silent, Irish, Harry, and his father left the road and went back toward the ranch, while the rest of the searchers went on toward Moolock. Silent and Irish lagged back during the ride across the hills.

"You ain't hoping to see her at home, are you?" asked Irish.

"Hoping, that's all, cowboy," replied Silent. "We had to bust up that argument somehow, Irish. It's a cinch that June got grabbed. Just who got her is a mystery. Me and you are going to Moolock after supper."

June was not at the ranch when they got there. Allenby's spirits went down below zero. He had evidently expected to find her there. Mrs. Allenby seemed very patient. She was not the kind of a woman to show great emotion. Harry came down to the bunkhouse, where Silent and Irish were getting ready for supper.

"I'm sorry," Harry said contritely. "That argument got on my nerves."

"That's all right," grinned Silent. "Maybe I'd have done the same thing. Just forget it, Harry."

"Well, I'm glad you feel that way about it," said Harry. "Pa seems to have great faith in you."

Silent smiled softly as he hung up his towel.

"Faith is a great thing, Harry," he said. "This whole world is built on faith. You can go a long ways if you have faith in yourself; but the minute you lose faith in yourself—you're done. And sometimes you're done when others lose faith in you."

"Are you a preacher?" asked Harry, a trifle sarcastically.

"A preacher?" Silent scowled thoughtfully. "No, I'm not a preacher, Harry. But maybe sometimes I repeat something smart I heard somewhere or read somewhere. That's all."

CHAPTER EIGHT

Lem Elder, a tall, weary-looking cowboy, who worked for Joe Bass of the 27A outfit, was singing as he rested his elbows on the White Horse Saloon bar.

Pete Sepulveda was sitting at a card table nearby, chin in hands, but now he looked up reprovingly at Lem.

"You hadn't ought to sing, Lem," he said seriously. "Songs ain't appreciated in Moolock tonight. You know, they ain't found that girl yet."

"That's right," nodded Lem. "Excuse me. That whisky they sell here makes you sing. Is anybody hunting for her, Pete?"

"Not now, I guess. Allenby and his bunch went home. Wasn't much they could do in the dark."

"I seen Harry and them two strange punchers ride in a while ago," said Pinon Meade, another of Joe Bass's men.

"That's Slade and O'Day," offered Pete. "They took the place of Omaha and Chet Hobson at the Half-Circle Cross."

"Hobson and Olsen get fired?" queried Lem.

"Yeah. Had a run-in with Allenby. They're still in town. They're two danged good cowhands."

"Where did Slade and O'Day come from?" asked Pinon.

"I don't know. Just drifted in, I suppose," said Pete.

"Good cowhands?" asked Lem.

"I'll bet you they are," grinned Pete.

Harry Allenby came in, his face flushed with drink. He ordered a whisky.

"Any news?" asked Pete anxiously.

"Not a thing," replied Harry, glancing toward the door. "Bud Bell is in town."

"Alone?" asked Pete.

"The old man and Sticky Clay are with him."

"Put your troubles in your war bag," advised Pete.

"You think I'm afraid of them?" Harry drained his glass and flipped it back on the bar. He was drunk enough to be reckless.

"I would be," said Lem Elder seriously.

"Hell, you fellows make me tired! I'll get them one at a time."

Pinon Meade laughed and walked out of the place. Harry's eyes snapped angrily. The strong liquor was percolating through his veins, taking away what little judgment he might have had. He rubbed the palm of his right hand on the butt of his revolver, and his lips were screwed into a sneering grin.

He did not notice that Pete and Lem had stepped away from him, nor that the bartender had moved

quietly toward the other end of the bar. He was
facing the door, squinting at the floor, and now he
looked up to see Sticky Clay framed in the doorway.

Harry blinked, as though not believing his eyes.
Clay did not move. Then Harry swayed away from
the bar, his right hand streaking for his gun. Harry
was fast with his draw, but not fast enough. The
experienced gunman in the doorway flipped his
hand forward, firing almost from the hip. Clay's
draw was almost too fast for the eye to follow.

Harry took a half step backward, dropped his
gun, and fell on his face, arms outspread. For several moments Clay leaned forward, watching him.
Then he straightened up, snapped his gun back in
the holster, and spoke to Pete.

"You saw this, Pete?"

Pete nodded quickly. "Yes, we all seen it, Sticky."

"Looking for it, wasn't he, Pete?" Clay said.

"He sure was."

"Got it, didn't he?"

Pete nodded.

"Everybody satisfied then?"

Sticky Clay turned and disappeared. Pete and
Lem turned Harry over, expecting to find him dead;
but he was far from it. The heavy bullet had creased
the top of one ear. He was bleeding freely, but
recovering nicely from the shock. A fraction of an
inch further to the right, and Harry Allenby would
have been a fatal casualty.

They helped him into a chair and bound his
head in a none-too-clean handkerchief. The report
of the gun had caused the curious to go searching
for its cause, with the result that Harry was soon
surrounded, and the White Horse Saloon began
doing a good business.

Swan River Smith investigated; he nodded over Pete Sepulveda's story, backed by Lem Elder. Silent Slade and Irish O'Day joined the crowd and listened to Pete closely.

"He was looking for trouble, Swan River," said Pete. "I don't blame Clay a bit. Harry started his draw first."

"And that settles it," said the sheriff. "As long as it was an even break."

Someone had gone for the doctor, who came and bandaged Harry's head in spite of Harry's protests that he did not need attention.

"You let him do it," said Clayton. "If you don't have it fixed up now, you'll be marked for life. You're damn lucky, Harry."

The shock had sobered Harry, and he had nothing to say. Silent and Irish crossed the street to the general store, where they found Hank and Bud Bell. Bud nodded to them. Several men were in the store, talking about the missing girl and about the stage robbery. Silent bought some peanuts and began to chew on them, when he saw Bud Bell signal him to come outside.

Bud sauntered out and in a few moments Silent followed him. Irish had seen the signal to Silent, but he did not go with his partner. Bud had walked down the walk out of the lights, and Silent joined him.

"Slade," Bud said without any preliminaries, "I want you to tell me all about this. I've heard several tales, but they are all different."

"Maybe mine is, too," said Silent, offering a peanut to Bud, who took one. "Anyway, here's how it looked to me."

He told Bud all he knew about the shooting of Shorty Elkins and the disappearance of June

Allenby. Bud did not interrupt. Silent told Bud his conclusions regarding the reasons for June's disappearance.

"Thank you, Slade," said Bud. "Do you remember Slim Stout?"

"Slim Stout?" Silent munched on a peanut for a moment, then nodded slowly. "Yes, I do. I sent him to the pen."

"That's where I met him, Slade. He told me about you."

"That's so, eh?"

"Yes. He's still got five years before he can look for a parole or a pardon. He says you let him off easy."

"Shell stuck in my gun," said Silent. "Slim didn't know it, I reckon."

Bud laughed shortly. "Slim didn't tell it that way."

"Likely lied to you. Now listen, Bell, as friend to friend, I want to warn you. Things are getting hotter every minute. Allenby has piled up evidence enough to hang a king—that is, outside the law. Sticky Clay and Harry Allenby just tried to kill each other a while ago in the White Horse, as you probably know. Allenby didn't get hurt much."

"As friend to friend?" said Bud wonderingly.

"Something like that."

"Why? Was it you who turned those two horses loose?"

"I needed the stable space," Silent lied.

"Yeah? And now you're working for Allenby?"

"Externally."

"Why are you taking an interest in me, Slade?"

"I don't know. Why does the wind blow? Ask me something easy. Now you take my advice and don't go to sleep. I know that all three of you are able to get along without crutches, but you can't buck the whole county. I'm doing all I can, Bell. If they hang you, that won't help me much, nor you either. I'm going to sneak out to see you just as soon as I can."

"I don't know what this is all about, but I'm all ears, Slade," said Bud. "We'll be awake all the time."

"Good. You've got something to live for."

"I can't figure you out," sighed Bell. "But thanks, Slade."

"Don't thank me."

Silent turned and walked up the street to the Elk Saloon, leaving Bud alone to think it over. More men were coming into town. Bud walked back to the store, signaled his father, and together they got their horses. They knew Sticky Clay had gone home after the shooting, to prevent any complications, which were bound to ensue if he stayed in town.

"Things look kinda cranky, Bud," observed the old man.

"Yeah, and I'm afraid they'll get worse, Pa. Stealing a girl is bad business. There's a lot of talk and a lot of whisky in Moolock tonight, so we better keep out of sight. I wish Sticky had kept away from Harry Allenby, but Harry was looking for it, and Clay is always willing to accommodate. They tell me that Harry started the draw first."

"Young Allenby is a fool to draw with Clay," observed the old man. "What did that tall cowpuncher want, Bud?"

"Wanted to give me some advice."

"He's working for Allenby, isn't he?"

"Yeah."

"Well, we don't need any advice from that damn outfit."

"This didn't come from that outfit, Pa. If it ever comes to a showdown, don't hurt that tall cowboy. And if he asks you to do something, do it."

"Who in blazes is he, Bud?"

"He turned the pinto and gray out of Swan River's stable."

"But he's working for Allenby, Bud."

"Yeah. I don't understand it, but I'm willing to follow his advice."

While the Bell men rode homeward, Silent went to the White Horse Saloon. Young Harry Allenby was still there, but fairly sober now. His head was bandaged and he was unable to wear his hat. Swan River took Silent aside and imparted the information that there was too much talk, mixed with whisky, to suit him.

"This girl-stealing has worked everybody up to a pitch," the sheriff declared. "Dang it, they'll ruin everything if they start out on a rampage. I've done a lot of talking, and I've kind of got some of them sore at me. Are Bud and Hank still in town?"

"Just left a few minutes ago," replied Silent. "I think Clay left just after the shooting."

More men came into the saloon. Silent and Swan River sat down at a vacant card table near the rear of the room. There they could watch the place. Silent fingered a deck of cards and made various designs as the sheriff watched him. Silent, his mind on the things that had happened, unconsciously maneuvered the cards around on the table.

Harry Allenby began drinking again and seemed to parade his bandages, talking loudly.

Silent glanced at him, then back to his cards.

Suddenly, he stopped fingering the cards and Swan River looked up into his eyes. There was a puzzled expression on Silent's face. He looked at the sheriff, a grin widening his mouth.

"What's the matter?" asked the sheriff.

"Do you still have that letter—the one that Seeley had in his pocket?"

The sheriff drew it out of an inside pocket and handed it to Silent, who spread it out on the table on top of his cards. For several minutes, Slade studied it closely, squinting away now and then at the action around the room. He was about to fold it up when something caused him to look at it again.

After concentrating on it for a space of time, he looked up at Swan River, a big grin on his face.

"What's so funny in that letter?" asked the sheriff.

"Nothing," replied Silent. "I was just thinking of something else. Mind if I keep this letter?"

Swan River shook his head. "It ain't no use to me."

Forty Dollar came in and walked straight to their table. Forty was serious as he sat down.

"Something is going to bust pretty soon," he declared. "Over at the Elk, they're talking too much to suit me. Some son-of-a-gun had told them about those two horses, and a few of the gang wants to know if the sheriff's office is standing in with the robbers."

Swan River's jaw clamped tightly and he got to his feet, hitching up his belt.

"I'll answer their danged questions," he rasped and started for the door. Clayton was coming in, and they almost collided. Clayton's sleeve was torn and he had the general appearance of one who had been fighting.

He stepped away from the sheriff and went to the bar, where he drank alone, turned his back against the bar, and looked around the room.

"Looks like friend Clayton had been fighting," observed Forty Dollar.

Forty's observation was punctuated with a zz-swhap! Clayton's shoulders thudded back against the bar and Silent went sideways out of his chair, while from outside came the report of a shot.

Clayton ducked, putting the end of the bar between himself and the open doorway, while the rest of the crowd scattered to get out of line. For several moments Clayton clawed at his shirt front. The bullet had burned across his chest, tearing a shallow furrow, but doing little damage, after which it passed within a short distance of Silent's head and thudded into the rear wall.

"Hurt you much?" asked Silent.

Clayton shook his head, sprang to his feet, and ran out the rear entrance. Disregarding a possible second shot, Silent and Forty Dollar ran through the front doorway and into the street. It was too dark, beyond the front window illumination, for them to see anyone.

Swan River came running from the Elk Saloon, followed by several men who had heard the shot. But the shooter had made himself scarce. Silent drew Swan River aside and together they made the rounds of the saloons, checking up on the cowboys. As far as they were able to find out, no one was missing, except Ed Clayton.

"Do you reckon they was trying to kill you, Slade,

or Clayton?" asked Irish, who joined them at the Elk.

"That's hard to tell, Irish. We'll figure it was Clayton. He'd had trouble with somebody just before the shot was fired. If we can find him, maybe he'll tell us who it was—if he knows."

But they were unable to find Ed Clayton, so Swan River opined that Clayton was hiding out. The folks of Moolock were getting plenty of food for conversation. Silent was curious about the trouble between Harry Allenby and Sticky Clay, so he found Pete Sepulveda and asked him about it again.

"Harry was looking for it, as I said before," grunted Pete, a trifle thickly. "Pinon Meade, Lem Elder, me, and Harry was there in the saloon when Harry got to making his war talk. Pinon pulled out and in a few seconds we happen to see Sticky in the doorway.

"Harry don't see him for a while, you see. Pretty soon he looks up and sees Sticky. They look at each other about a second and Harry breaks for his gun. Sticky makes his draw, shoots from the hip, and Harry falls on his nose. Sticky thinks he's killed Harry, I reckon; but he ain't excited. It was an even break, that's all."

"Much obliged, Pete," said Silent thoughtfully. "Has there ever been any trouble between Harry and Pinon Meade?"

"I don't reckon there was. Pinon ain't quarrelsome."

Silent drifted back to Swan River and Irish. And he found Frank Allenby listening to Swan River tell about the gun battle between Harry and Sticky Clay. Allenby had little to say. He seemed to have aged greatly in the last few hours.

Silent drew him aside. "Has there ever been any trouble between you and Pinon Meade?" asked Silent.

"Not at all," replied Allenby. "Why do you ask?"

"Just wondering, that's all," said Silent. "You heard about someone shooting at Clayton, haven't you?"

Allenby nodded quickly. "Yes, but I do not understand it. I can't find Clayton anywhere. He is not at the hotel."

"There's a fly in the axle-grease somewhere," mused Silent.

"I don't know what you mean, nor what to do," said Allenby. "I can't stand it much longer. My wife just sits and looks at the wall. I wish she would cry. It helps a woman to cry. Don't you think so, Slade?"

"Not as much as it does to laugh, Allenby. I want to ask you a very personal question: Is Clayton going to marry your daughter?"

"What has that to do—"

"I'm asking—not answering, Allenby."

"I suppose he is—what about it?"

"Is there anyone else who might want June bad enough to kill Clayton over her?" asked Silent.

Allenby took a deep breath and shut his jaw tightly for a moment.

"Do you suppose that is why he tried to kill Clayton?"

"He? Who do you mean, Allenby?" Slade asked.

But Allenby refused to say. Harry went past them, his bandaged head visible in the weak light, and went into the Elk Saloon. He staggered slightly, laughing loudly with the other men. Allenby left Silent and went into the saloon.

Silent and Irish went from place to place, listening to the general talk. It was mostly whisky conversation, and Silent did not feel that the men were going to do anything rash. Later on he found Swan River again, visibly relieved.

"I think everything will be all right," the sheriff said. "I've talked with a few of them, including Allenby, and they've all agreed to wait until morning. I've promised to lead a posse out to the HB ranch after daylight. If they—well, I don't know. Dang it, I've done the best I could, boys."

"Nobody can say that you haven't been fair," agreed Silent.

"Maybe I've been too fair, Slade. Still, I discount everything that happens when there's hate behind it. Winter hated old Hank Bell. Maybe Allenby bought that hate along with the ranch."

"How did they happen to catch Bud Bell that other time?" asked Silent.

"When they sent him to the penitentiary? That was a little over two years ago. Allenby and Clayton—Clayton had only been here a few months at that time—were riding through the hills, looking over stock.

"They were over near Two Men Canyon when they caught a glimpse of a man who kind of seemed to be misbranding a couple of critters. Had them roped and was heating his iron, I reckon. Anyway, he seen them, too, so he snaps out of the brush on his horse and heads into the hills, with Allenby and Clayton after him.

"He sure led them a merry chase, I guess. Allenby and Clayton got separated, and after a while they gave up the chase. Clayton circles back to the two roped animals and is looking at them when Allenby gets back. They're both branded fresh with the HB iron, kind of roughlike, and

where the Half-Circle Cross ought to be is a big
spot burned half over with a hot fry-pan.

"The rustler sure must have been nervous to
burn over that much space in venting an ordinary
brand. The HB ain't very artistic, but there she
is. That was all the evidence against Bud Bell. Old
Hank couldn't have done it, on account of being
crippled—and Sticky Clay was in a poker game
in Moolock all afternoon, which was an alibi for
him. So they sent Bud up for stealing Half-Circle
Cross stock."

"Didn't Bud have any defense at all?"

"How could he? Nobody would steal cattle for
the HB. You know, Bud used to wear one of them
five-gallon hats with a wide band, kind of studded
with silver rosettes. Oh, you could see it a mile
away, glistening in the sun. Anyway, both Allenby
and Clayton testified that this rustler wore no hat.
Allenby says he was sure the man had a hat when
he seen him first, but that he was bareheaded
when he made his getaway.

"Allenby says he was too excited to remember
just what kind of a hat this man had on when he
seen him first. But it made things worse for Bud.
He'd naturally hide the hat, because it was so well-
known and easy to identify."

"They didn't get close enough to identify him
for sure?"

"Nope. But their evidence sure convinced the
jury," sighed Swan River, shaking his head.

"The Half-Circle Cross brands on the right
shoulder, and the HB on the right hip, don't they?"
asked Silent.

"Yeah," nodded the sheriff. "Bud sure vented a
lot of space on the right shoulder of them two critters."

"No argument about them being Half-Circle Cross animals?"

"There might have been, Slade, but you could look real close and find the old scars of the original brand. They'd have never showed up after a few days, when the new burns healed. No, there was no question about them being Allenby's stock."

"And the vented spot was much bigger than the old brand, eh?"

"Hell, yes, four or five times bigger," grunted Swan River.

"Uh-huh." Silent grew thoughtful. "And you think there's no danger of anybody doing anything rash tonight, Sheriff?"

"Nope. They'll likely drink a lot of liquor and kind of gird up their loins, but that's about all. Will you ride out to the HB with us in the morning?"

"Very likely. I reckon we'll go back to the ranch and get a little sleep now."

Irish complained about leaving Moolock. It looked to Irish as though there might be trouble, and he did not want to miss any of it. He grumbled audibly but rode out of town with Silent.

"I suppose," he said sarcastically, "that old folks like you have got to have their sleep, Silent."

"You betcha," agreed Silent. "And so do wounded men. You seem to forget your wounded shoulder."

"Aw, it's all right," grunted Irish.

"Irish, do you think you can find the HB ranch?"

"Yeah, I can find it. What's the idea?"

"Going visiting, Irish. Folks ought to be neighborly, hadn't they?"

"At this time of night?" said Irish. "The road runs kinda southeast; so we better swing to the

left. What are we going to do out there? Didn't
Swan River say that he was—"

"Going out there after daylight," said Silent.
"That's the trouble with the ordinary sheriff, Irish,
they want to make a parade out of it. They never
find out anything."

"What do you expect to find out?"

"Pardner, you never know what to expect. Anyway, we're going out that way and see what we'll
see," said Silent. "Probably won't see anything—
maybe.we will."

"Uh-huh," Irish grunted dubiously, but he knew
Silent and knew better than to ask too many questions. "What was the idea of all them questions
about Bud stealing cows and getting sent to the
pen?"

"Morbid curiosity, Irish. I just love to hear about
grief and misery."

"Oh, go to blazes!" snorted Irish.

"Very likely—if there is such a place, Irish."

CHAPTER NINE

No lights were visible at the HB ranch house when Silent Slade and Irish O'Day swung in behind the buildings, silhouetted in the moonlight. Silent felt that somewhere around that black hulk of buildings someone was watching. They dismounted and led their horses away from the road into a clump of trees, which would screen them from anyone passing on the way to the ranch or from it.

"Got to get higher," said Silent as he led the way out of the trees, keeping well away from the ranch, circling toward a rise of ground back of the stable. They were forced to proceed at a slow pace for fear of running into loose barbed wire or other unknown difficulties.

At last they reached a point where they could look down on the group of buildings, and here they sat to wait. It was well after midnight when they reached this point, and an hour later there was sufficient moonlight to enable them to distinguish the buildings more clearly and the contour of the surrounding country.

For a long time there was no sound, except for the soft bawling of a cow. Far out in the hills a coyote called mournfully, and from the house came the short bark and growl of a dog. Then all was still again. Hour after hour went past, while the two cowboys huddled in the sage, unmoving, both of them tired and hungry.

The false dawn lighted the hills and a chill wind swept down the canyon, causing the two cowboys to sink lower into the protecting brush. Suddenly, Silent sat up. The dim figure of a man had crossed the corrals and faded into the shadows of the stable.

"Did you see him?" asked Silent softly.

"Yeah," shivered Irish. "He went into the stable. Probably one of the HB outfit doing his chores early. Of all the fools on earth, we're the worst. Sitting out here in the cold all night. There he goes back again."

The man crossed the corrals again, going in the opposite direction. He either went through a gate or crawled through the fence and blended with the shadows so well that they were unable to see him again. They listened to see if they could hear him shut a door in the house, but there was no sound.

After several minutes, the dog barked loudly, and from the hills came the snapping bark of a coyote. The dog, evidently under leash, grew frantic with its barking; but the coyote did not respond. Silent chuckled softly.

"What's so danged funny?" asked Irish.

"That coyote."

"What in blazes is funny about a coyote?"

"Well, that particular one probably smokes cigarettes and packs a six-gun."

"You mean that wasn't a coyote, Silent?"

"That's what I mean," Slade said.

"But why would any man imitate a coyote that way?" Irish asked.

"To make the dog bark."

"Oh, I see," snorted Irish sarcastically. He was chilled to the bone and hungry. "Why in blazes would he want to make a dog bark, if I may ask?"

"So that anybody would think he was barking at a coyote."

"All right, all right," groaned Irish, feeling his hurt shoulder. "Someday I'm going to ask you a question and get an intelligent answer."

"And what then, Irish?"

"The shock will kill me."

Silent laughed softly and got to his feet. "Let's sneak down there and see what that jigger was doing. He never went into the house, so I don't figure he's part and parcel of the HB."

Cautiously they made their way down the hill and came in behind the stable. Daylight was coming swiftly now, but there was no sign of the man who had crossed the corrals. They slid through the corral fence, circled the interior until they were opposite the door to the stable. There they again passed through the fence.

Part of a long, low shed blocked their view of the house.

"Wait here and keep watch," whispered Silent. "I'm going inside."

Irish crouched against the fence, while Silent opened the stable door and went inside. He was in there so long that Irish became nervous. It was daylight now, and Irish felt like a burglar. He turned his head and looked toward the road. Only a few hundred yards away, coming up the road, was a big group of horsemen.

"That sheriff's posse!" snorted Irish. He ran to the stable door to notify Silent, and met him coming out.

"Swan River and his men are here!" he blurted. "Whatsa matter? Did you go to sleep in there?"

Silent ran to the corner of the stable and watched the horsemen swing in toward the ranch house.

"C'mon," he whispered, running straight back toward the hill, keeping the stable between them and the ranch house. Irish was at his heels, and together they tumbled into a shallow wash behind some old wild rosebushes.

"We can get back to our horses by going down this wash," said Silent. "Keep your head down and c'mon."

It did not take them long to get their horses, swing back into the road, and head for the ranch house. The posse was grouped at the ranch-house door, talking with Old Hank, Bud, and Sticky Clay. Swan River had dismounted and was leaning against the porch, but the rest of the riders were still in their saddles.

They turned and looked as Silent and Irish rode up to them.

"Missed you in town, Sheriff," said Silent.

The sheriff nodded and turned to Hank Bell. "I'm not charging you with anything, Hank. I want you to understand that right here. There's been so much talk that I had an idea that we ought to come out here this morning and find out how much of it was worth arguing about."

Old Hank squinted at the posse, which was composed of Jack Merton, Pete Sepulveda, Frank Allenby, Joe Bass, Larry Neil, Forty Dollar, Lem Elder, Omaha Olsen, and Chet Hobson.

"Well," said Old Hank slowly, "what do you want to do?" He seemed curiously meek, weary.

"Just to satisfy everybody, suppose we search the place," suggested Swan River.

Old Hank squinted closely at Swan River, as though wondering what they expected to find.

"Go ahead," said Bud slowly. "I reckon we can stand for that."

Old Hank nodded in agreement, and the posse dismounted.

"We'll help you, if you need help," grinned Sticky Clay.

Old Hank threw open the front door, and the posse filed inside, led by Swan River. Silent and Irish did not go in with them, but sat down on the little porch. It did not take long to search the house, and then the posse split into two groups, to search the stable and other outbuildings.

Silent followed now, and helped them go over every inch of the place. For about an hour they stayed at the HB, leaving no stone unturned in their efforts to uncover some evidence.

But their time was wasted and they came back to their horses.

"Satisfied?" asked Bud.

Swan River nodded as he swung into his saddle.

"Yeah, I'm satisfied, Bud—and I hope the rest are."

The rest of them did not express an opinion. Allenby slumped in his saddle, paying little attention to anyone during the ride back to town.

He had hoped to find June at the HB ranch.

"You never find girl there," said Joe Bass. "Bell's no fool. We find nothing there."

"That's the way I felt about it," said Swan River. "If Bell did rob the stage and steal the girl, he wouldn't put her in a showcase for us to see. This idea of going out in a crowd is all foolishness, I tell you."

"That's right," nodded Joe Bass.

Allenby, Silent, and Irish did not stop in Moolock, but rode on to the Half-Circle Cross, intending to get breakfast at the ranch.

"I wish I knew what to do," said Allenby wearily. "There is no clue, nothing to work on. The sheriff is right when he says that those who stole June won't keep her where we can find her. If they want money—"

"I don't reckon they do," said Silent. "I know how you feel, Allenby. I know how your wife must feel about it; but it's something that can't be helped right now. Did you see anything of Clayton after he got shot last night?"

"No, I didn't see him, but Harry did. He told Harry he was going to the ranch. I think someone tried to kill him and that he was frightened into leaving Moolock."

"Harry had a close call, too," observed Irish.

Allenby nodded sadly, but did not express an opinion. It seemed as though his hatred of the HB outfit had burned out, or had burned him out.

Mrs. Allenby came from the house to meet them, hoping that they brought news, but she was doomed to disappointment. She did not speak. Allenby turned his horse over to Silent to unsaddle and walked up to the house with her.

Silent and Irish stabled the horses and walked

back to the bunkhouse. Clayton was sitting on the porch of the ranch house.

"Well, we're just as wise as we were before we went to the HB," grunted Irish, stretching himself out on his bunk. "Lost one whole night's sleep and didn't gain a darned thing. That was probably one of the HB outfit that crossed the corrals this morning."

"I don't hardly think so," said Silent, yawning wearily. "It wasn't none of the HB outfit that barked like a coyote."

"Aw, shucks!" Irish did not believe that a man had barked like a coyote.

"Well, the dog barked," said Silent.

"Yeah, the dog barked. He was tied up."

"And if the coyote hadn't barked, some of the HB would have come out to see why the dog barked, wouldn't they?"

Irish sat up and scratched his head thoughtfully.

"Yeah, I suppose so, Silent."

"The coyote barked first, didn't it? Then the man crossed the corral. After he left, the coyote barked closer, didn't he? And the dog barked again, at the coyote."

"Well, what has the coyote got to do with it? What had the man to do with it? You always make a lot out of nothing, Silent. You make me lose a whole night's sleep and then you make boogers out of a man crossing a corral, or a coyote that sounds like a man. What good did it do us?"

Silent walked to the window and looked toward the house. Allenby was sitting on the ranch-house porch, talking to Clayton, and there was no one else in sight. Silent turned and came back to Irish's bunk.

He reached inside his shirt and drew out two flat envelopes covered with seals, which had been broken: two empty manila envelopes, which had been shipped as valuable packages by an express company. Irish took them in his hands and looked them over closely.

"I had an awful time finding them in that stable," said Silent as he took them back and slipped them back inside his shirt. "They were under a currycomb and brush in a little box on the wall."

"That's some of the loot from the train robbery," whispered Irish.

"They once held some of the loot," corrected Silent.

"But the posse couldn't find anything."

"There wasn't anything left," said Silent.

Irish squinted at the ceiling thoughtfully. "Silent, who searched that box on the wall?"

Silent grinned widely and shook his head. "Swan River Smith did. These Moolock outlaws ain't fools, cowboy. Now will you believe that a man barked like a coyote, Irish?"

"Hell, I'd believe that they buzzed like a rattler, if you say so. Right now I'm in the right frame of mind to believe anything. Have you got any clue, Silent, anything to work on? Oh, no, you wouldn't say so, if you had a million clues."

"Yeah, I've got a clue, but I can't tell you what it is."

"All right. Keep me ignorant."

"Don't blame me for what nature done to you, Irish. Let's snore a few lines, whatcha say? Maybe we'll need it."

"I can always do that, pardner. Sleep is my first name."

* * *

While Silent and Irish slumbered in the bunk-house, Allenby and Clayton sat on the ranch-house porch and the rancher told Clayton about their failure to secure any evidence against the HB out-fit. He told of the search and of Hank Bell's will-ingness to have them search the place.

"He's no fool," grumbled Clayton. "He's been expecting trouble for a long time, and he surely wouldn't take a chance on having any incrimi-nating evidence in sight. If he and his outfit robbed that stage and kidnapped June, they wouldn't take her to the ranch."

"No, I suppose not, Clayton. Have you any idea who shot you?"

"Not in the least." Clayton shook his head as he felt his bandages where the bullet had scored his breastbone.

"You haven't had any trouble with anyone, have you?"

Clayton shook his head again. "Not a bit of it. The only person who might have done it would be that fellow, Clay, who shot Harry."

"Did you have any trouble with Clay?"

"Not a bit. I just thought perhaps he might be sore at all of us. I have been out here so much of the time they seem to think that I'm one of the Half-Circle Cross outfit."

"I suppose so," said Allenby dubiously. "Still, it is hardly reasonable, Clayton. Sticky Clay is a gunman, and I don't think he would try to murder you in cold blood."

"Well, pick a more likely suspect." Clayton was angered a little over Allenby's words. "I've thought about it until I can't arrive at any conclusion. Perhaps that bullet was intended for Slade. It didn't miss him by far."

"That might be possible, too. Where is Harry?"

"He went back to town this morning after breakfast. Did Slade and O'Day ride with the posse?"

"They got there after we did. What time did they leave here this morning?" asked Allenby.

"They didn't sleep here last night."

"Didn't they? That's queer. Swan River Smith said they'd gone back to the ranch. They didn't stay in Moolock."

"Well, they didn't stay here," declared Ed Clayton. "Harry and I slept in the bunkhouse." He turned his chair and looked at Allenby as he lowered his voice. "Do you know much about these two men?"

Allenby nodded slowly. "I know what Freeman told me. He said Slade was the shrewdest cattle detective that ever wore a gun. I am not going to question what they do, Clayton. If they wanted to tell the sheriff that they were coming here to the ranch last night, and went elsewhere—that's their business."

"But you didn't hire them as detectives?"

"I did not. But I told them both that my former offer of five thousand dollars for a conviction still stands, and that they could do as they pleased while on the job."

"Well, that's different," nodded Clayton. "I just didn't understand the arrangement. I think I'll go back to town and see if anything new has turned up. Want to go along?"

"Not now, Ed."

Allenby went into the house, while Clayton, deep in thought, went to the stable, saddled his horse, and rode toward Moolock.

* * *

It was midafternoon when Silent and Irish awoke. They could hear someone talking outside, so Silent slipped to the window and looked out. It was Omaha Olsen and Chet Hobson. Silent and Irish went out to meet them.

"Anything new in town?" asked Silent.

"Nothing," replied Hobson. "We got tired sitting around, so we thought we'd take a ride ourselves and see what we could find."

"So far, we haven't found much," grunted Omaha. "We got this far and found almost everyone gone. Didn't know you boys were here."

"Saw Mrs. Allenby sitting on the porch," said Hobson. "I sure feel for her."

"Seems kinda funny to me that none of the other women folks around this country have come in to weep with Mrs. Allenby," observed Irish.

"Ain't nothing funny about it," declared Omaha. "Allenby is to blame for it all. He's been so danged uppity, that's all. He ain't never fit in with regular folks. Thinks he's worth more than they are."

"Don't make friends, eh?" queried Silent.

"Don't make nothing but money," said Omaha.

"And somebody steals the profits," grunted Hobson. "Well, reckon we'll move on. See you later."

Silent and Irish watched them ride away. Then they went up to the ranch house where Cookie offered to fix something for them to eat, which they accepted.

After satisfying their appetites, Irish went back to the bunkhouse while Silent went toward the front of the house. He discovered Mrs. Allenby standing there, looking off across the hills, shading her eyes. He studied her for a moment before coming up to the porch. She lowered her hand from her eyes and looked at Silent.

"I—I was just looking," she said simply.

"Yes'm," nodded Silent. "The hills are kind of pretty this time of day."

"Pretty?" She shook her head slowly. "I didn't notice—much."

"Where is Mr. Allenby?"

"I think he went to town."

"Oh, yeah, I suppose he did."

"I wish Harry would come home. He stays away most of the time these days. Where do you suppose June is?"

"I don't know, ma'am. It's all kind of mixed up. Clayton was going to marry June, wasn't he?"

Mrs. Allenby stared at Silent, and a little color came into her white cheeks.

"Who told you that?" she asked.

"I don't remember. It wasn't a secret, was it, Mrs. Allenby?"

"No, I—I don't know." She shook her head slowly. "Mr. Allenby wouldn't—"

"He didn't want Clayton for a son-in-law, eh?"

"Did he tell you that?"

"No, he didn't, Mrs. Allenby. Would you want him?"

"Mr. Clayton?"

"Yes," Silent said.

"Why, I—what right have you to ask me a question of that kind?"

"Mrs. Allenby, I don't want to pry into your secrets, but I've got to know a few things. If you want your daughter back—"

"Oh, but I do!" Mrs. Allenby gripped the porch post and stared at Silent. "I would sacrifice anything to get June home again."

"Sure you would. You'll get her, ma'am; but you've got to have a lot of patience. Now I want you to answer me this: Does June want to marry Ed Clayton?"

She turned away, shaking her head.

"All right. But you've done quite a lot to convince her that she ought to marry him, ain't you?" Silent prodded.

Mrs. Allenby turned quickly and stared at him. "What makes you say that?" she stammered.

"Because it is true." Silent knew that his guess had been correct.

"Now you're going to tell me why you wanted June to marry Clayton."

"How did you find out these things?" Mrs. Allenby's face was white, but her voice did not tremble now. "Who told you?"

"Nobody. Maybe I read it in the clouds. I just want you to tell me why you promoted Clayton."

"Promoted him?"

"Well, something like that. Go ahead and talk about it."

For several moments Silent was afraid that she was going to rebel. Finally, she sat down in a rocking chair near him, and he knew that the point was won.

"It was the wrong thing to do," she began slowly. "But you do not know my husband. His one ambition is having more money. All his life he has been a slave to money. No, I am not complaining, nor excusing myself. I did wrong and I'll admit everything I have done.

"Ed Clayton has wanted to marry June ever since he first came here to buy cattle. June did not seem to care for him. Mr. Allenby liked him as a cattle-buyer, but he didn't want him to marry June. I did not dislike Ed Clayton. He was a gentleman, until..."

Mrs. Allenby shook her head sadly.

"At any rate he asked Mr. Allenby for June's hand and was refused. It did not seem to make any difference to Clayton. He told me about it and asked me to speak up for him. I knew it was useless. When Mr. Allenby makes up his mind to a thing, nothing can change him.

"I told Mr. Clayton that it would not help his case in any way. He and Harry were great friends, so Harry came and asked me to help Clayton out. Harry liked Ed, who always had money. You know, Harry never has any money. His father does not believe in giving children much money—and he does not realize that Harry and June have grown up.

"Later I began to hear stories about Harry. They said that he was drinking and gambling. I know that his father heard the same stories, but he merely laughed and proved to me that it was all lies, because Harry had almost no money to drink and gamble with.

"Ed Clayton knew that I idolized my children. He knew that I would go to any length to help them. So one day he came to me and asked me to see if I couldn't help him win June. I gave him the same answer. He did not get angry, nor did he threaten; but he did show me receipts for borrowed money, a total of five thousand dollars, signed with Harry's name.

"Clayton had loaned Harry all that money. Clayton knew what Mr. Allenby would do if he knew that Harry had done such a thing. But Clayton did not threaten me. He just pointed out the fact that someone must pay back that money. He had loaned it in good faith. He said to me, 'Mrs. Allenby, I love June more than anything in the world, and I will try to make her happy. I feel sure that a little urging will win for me. And, in that event, I will give you these receipts, and everything will be forgotten.'

"That is why I tried to—oh, I know it was wrong, but—"

"Yeah, it was all wrong, Mrs. Allenby," agreed Silent.

"But my urging did not help." Mrs. Allenby was crying now. "And I am glad. It would have been like selling my Junie. I realized that afterwards, but at the time I could only see what might happen to Harry. Don't you see?"

"Yes, I see," nodded Silent, getting to his feet. "I'm sure obliged to you, ma'am. This here is a secret between us."

"Oh, I hope so," said the woman. "I don't know why I told it all to you."

"That's all right, ma'am," grinned Silent. "Look for the silver lining. It's there."

She squinted at him and tried to smile.

Silent turned and left the porch and walked back to the bunkhouse where he found Irish on the porch.

"What were you and the lady chewing about, Silent?"

"Arguing about raising chickens. She favored one breed and I held out for another."

"And she cried for her side, eh? Yeah, I seen her wipe her eyes. You can lie faster than I can, Silent."

Silent grinned and headed for the stable, where they saddled their horses and started for town.

They found Forty Dollar Dion at the sheriff's office, bewailing everything.

"Swan River has led out another posse," he told them. "He's got Allenby, Sepulveda, Merton, Neil, and a couple of men from town riding with him. They're heading for Tecoma. Don't know where in hell they're going, but they're going, that's all. Swan River made me stay here, dang his hide. Said somebody had to protect the office."

Forty did not get much sympathy from Silent and Irish, so he paraded the rest of his woes, thusly:

"Ed Clayton is drunk and wants to fight somebody, the big brute. Harry Allenby is drunk enough to brag again, and he wants to help Clayton whip somebody, and there ain't nobody around here to accommodate them. Pinon Meade might fight the two of them, if he gets drunk enough; but Clayton, alone, is twice as big as Pinon. So there you are. On account of my official position, I can't fight them. Any news of the lost girl?"

Silent grinned at Forty Dollar's woes and shook his head.

"No news, Forty. You heard anything?"

"How the devil could I, sitting here all the time? It ain't none of my business," he added pointedly, "but I was just wondering where you two fellows were when we rode up to the HB this morning?"

Silent lifted his eyebrows slightly, but his expression remained the same. Then a smile wreathed his face.

"What makes you ask that question, Forty?"

"Curiosity. We was late getting started, and we sure did whang the blazes out of our horses all the way. We never passed you on the road, and when you came up to us, your horses wasn't even breathing hard."

"Forty Dollar," grinned Silent, "you're a born detective."

"Yeah? Well, I do notice some things. I kind of had a hunch that you fellows was poking around. Swan River wondered why you wasn't there to join the posse, and I told him that you wasn't the kind to run in packs."

"I reckon that's true," laughed Silent. "Swan River didn't say when he'd be back, did he?"

"He didn't know. Everybody expects him to be heading a searching party, so he's doing it."

They invited Forty Dollar to go across to the Elk with them, but he declined. Swan River had told him to stay at the office, which meant in town, but Forty Dollar translated it literally.

Harry Allenby was at the Elk, still wearing his bandages, which were slightly disarranged, and he was more than partly drunk. Silent took him aside and advised him to go home, but Harry would have none of Silent's advice.

"You ain't running my business," he said angrily. "I do as I please."

"That's your whole trouble," said Silent. "You're just a fool kid, without brains enough to pound sand into a rat-hole. You go on home and quit spending money that don't belong to you."

The shot went home! Harry's eyes blinked for a moment and he had difficulty in swallowing, but he tried to bluff.

"What in blazes do you mean by that?" he demanded.

"You know what I mean, Harry. If you want me to tell you, I'll tell it loud enough for everyone to hear."

"Who told you that?" Harry's voice was hoarse with anxiety.

"Who told me what?"

"That—that—" Harry hesitated, trying to clear

his thoughts. "That I was spending money that didn't belong to me," he finished lamely. "It's a lie."

"It's the truth, kid." Silent spoke softly and with conviction. "Your mother wants you to come home."

"Aw!" Harry turned away and walked outside.

There were only a few men in the Elk at this time of day. Three punchers were playing a card game at one of the tables, while Snowy Barnette and a railroad contractor were playing two-handed stud at the bar. Silent and Irish drifted over to the pool table and began playing bottle pool.

Their game was about half finished when Harry came back, and with him was Ed Clayton. Clayton had been drinking, but he was not drunk. He and Harry had a drink together and were at the bar when Silent and Irish put up their cues.

Silent noticed that both of them were serious, and as Silent approached the bar, Clayton stepped in front of him. In spite of Silent's height, Clayton was a half head taller and weighed at least fifty pounds more.

"Who in blazes told you that I loaned Harry money?" he demanded.

Silent glared coldly at Clayton and said evenly: "I didn't say you did, Clayton."

"You didn't?" Clayton whirled on Harry. "Didn't you say he told you that, Harry?"

"Why, I—I—that's what he meant, Ed. He didn't—"

Clayton turned back to Silent. "Where did you get this misinformation, Slade?"

"I don't reckon I was misinformed," smiled Silent easily. "It kind of looks like Harry had proved it. I didn't say who he got the money from—but he did."

"Is that so?" Clayton sneered openly. "Well, I just want to tell you that it's none of your damn business, Slade. You are taking too much for granted, and I want you to keep your nose out of my business, or I'll bust it wide open."

"Your business?" asked Silent innocently. "That won't take much, because it's already beginning to crack."

Clayton was rather a sudden sort of person, and believed in the theory that the first punch wins. This tall, skinny puncher was only three feet away, slouched easily, when Clayton's left fist snapped straight for his jaw. But that easy slouch was misleading, and allowed Silent to sway aside while the blow merely swished into empty air.

Silent did not lift his hands, but he did step back with a grin on his lips. Clayton blinked and recovered his balance. It was the first time he had missed with the snappy left, which was his stock in trade and usually put him in a good position to finish the fight without much opposition.

The card games ceased immediately. Harry started forward, only to have Irish kick his feet from under him and drop him in a sitting position half under a table.

"Get a front seat!" grunted Irish.

Clayton forced a smile to cover his chagrin. He did not expect this cowpuncher to put up a fight.

"You hadn't ought to telegraph your punch," grinned Silent. "A one-punch fighter like you ought to figure out a system, Clayton. You tried to sneak one on me, but your eyes and the whole left side of you told me what you were going to do."

"Did, eh?" Clayton smiled grimly as he fell into a crouch. "Stop this one!" He darted at Silent, smashing with both hands.

It was a disastrous attack. His right fist snapped against the top of Silent's head, the left missed entirely, and Clayton went backward, half doubled up from a punishing smash in the stomach.

He backed out of range, his mouth wide open, as he tried to pump air into his lungs. Silent laughed and shook his head.

"Go in and get him, cowboy!" called Irish. "He's whipped right now!"

"Like hell he is!" snorted Clayton, shutting his teeth and trying to strain the kinks out of his midriff.

"Well, come on and finish it," invited Silent. "If I want to whip you, I'd have stopped the fight before this; but it ain't no fight of my making."

Clayton was game, but wary. He had tasted one of Silent's rough punches and did not care for another of the same kind, so he elected to try the long-range game. He felt that this cowpuncher knew nothing about boxing. Someone shoved a table away to give them more room, and Harry Allenby crawled on his hands and knees to the bar rail, where he sat down, closely watched by Irish.

Clayton went in slowly, balanced easily on the balls of his feet, his guard high. Silent watched him calmly, guard down. It seemed to anger Clayton to think that this lanky person did not take the fight seriously enough to put up his hands.

Clayton stepped in range, snapping his left at Silent's head. It was rather a weak attempt and Silent avoided it easily as he stepped inside the blow, blocked Clayton's right, and drove another punch to Clayton's middle section.

It was enough to cause Clayton to drop his guard and step back, but this time the lanky cowboy stepped with him, and before Clayton could lift a

hand to stop it, Silent uppercut him to the point
of the jaw, with a full sweeping blow—and the
fight ended.

Clayton collapsed heavily, rolled over on his
back, and stared at the ceiling.

"The most complete thing I ever seen," declared
Snowy Barnette, walking to the fallen man. "I
knew that Clayton would get whipped someday;
but I thought it would take a bigger man than he
is."

The bartender threw a little water into Clayton's face, and he sat up, gasping. It was a full
minute before he realized what had happened. He
got painfully to his feet, leaned on the bar for a
while, trying to regain his balance. Then Ed Clayton walked outside without a word. Harry Allenby
followed him, rather disconsolately. His idol had
fallen—and fallen hard.

"I've paid twenty dollars to see a fight that wasn't
half as good," declared the railroad man. "Here's
to one cowpuncher that don't need to shoot his man
to win."

CHAPTER TEN

"Just my darned luck!" wailed Forty Dollar Dion. "Here I been laying on my miserable back, reading *Deserted at the Altar,* while there's a fight just across the street. That ain't no way to treat a friend. And Silent knocked out Ed Clayton, eh? Can't get it through my head, that's all. Bigger'n Silent, every way."

"Don't know the first thing about fighting," declared Irish. "Clumsy as a cub bear. Silent slapped him in the stomach and took all the fight out of him. Yellow as a dandelion."

"I seen him put up some pretty good fights," said Forty Dollar. "What did Harry think of the fight?"

"I kicked him into a front-row seat," said Irish. "When they tackle old Silent, there ain't but one decision to give. He just pets them on the chin, that's all."

"Bragging is bad; but lying and bragging at the same time is worse," declared Silent. "Your loop is dragging."

"It all sounds good to me," grinned Forty.

"Are you familiar with the 27A brand?" asked Silent.

"What do you want to know about the 27A?"

"Where do they brand?"

"Right shoulder," replied Forty. "The 7 and the A are connected."

"Uh-huh," nodded Silent as he walked to the doorway. He could see Ed Clayton and Harry Allenby in front of the White Horse Saloon, and as he watched them, Clayton drew back his right hand and knocked Harry into the street.

It was not a knockout punch, but it sent Harry rolling into the dust. He clawed his way to his feet and went staggering across the street. Silent called Irish and Forty Dollar to the doorway and told them about it.

Clayton went back into the saloon while Harry sat down on the walk in front of the general store.

"Harry seems to get it from all sides," observed Forty Dollar. "His luck is running kind of low this week."

Harry leaned against the hitchrack post and seemed content to stay where he was. In a few minutes Pinon Meade came out of the White Horse, got his horse, and rode out of town toward the 27A. The three men in the sheriff's office doorway went back inside and sat down.

Silent sat at the sheriff's desk and made pencil notes on the back of a piece of paper that had already been scribbled upon. Irish and Forty Dollar sat and watched him.

"He gets that way once in a while," said Irish.

"Don't bother him or ask him any questions, because he'll plumb ignore you."

Silent fooled around with some marks on the paper. Then, with a smile on his face, he folded the paper and shoved it into his pocket just as Swan River and his posse returned to Moolock. Their long ride had netted them nothing. They had come back past the 27A where Joe Bass had left them. Frank Allenby was discouraged. He asked for Harry and found that the young man had gone home.

Clayton, showing no ill effects from his fight, talked with Allenby, after which he got his horse and they rode away toward the ranch. Swan River stretched his tired body and swore witheringly at his luck.

"I reckon Allenby is all broken up," he said. "But I can't help it. I tried."

"Let's eat," suggested Forty Dollar. And as they headed for the restaurant, he told the tired sheriff about the two fights that had taken place.

Swan River nodded, but made no comment, as he didn't believe his deputy. He thought it was all a joke until they got inside the restaurant where he heard two men talking about Silent knocking out Clayton.

"I didn't know that there was trouble between you and Clayton," said Swan River as they sat down.

"There wasn't," smiled Silent. "He just wanted to fight."

"Uh-huh." Swan River was a bit dubious over this.

He knew that something must have been of sufficient import to cause such a battle, but he was willing to outwardly accept Silent's explanation.

After supper they wandered into the Elk where they ran into Sticky Clay, who was perfectly sober. He drew Silent aside from the others.

"You ain't seen Bud Bell, have you?" he asked.

"Nope—not since we were out there this morning."

"He ain't been here today, eh?"

"I don't think so. Anyway, I haven't seen him. What's wrong?"

"Bud rode away just after the posse left the HB, and he ain't come back. Me and the old man was kind of worried."

"Bud can take care of himself," Slade said.

"Ordinarily," conceded Sticky. "I suppose he's all right. You see, Slade, I think a lot of Bud."

Silent nodded. "Clay, I want to ask you something."

"Ask me anything."

"About that mixup between you and Harry Allenby. Did you know that Harry was gunning for you?"

"Well, yeah, you might say I did. He was just drunk enough to be looking for trouble. Somebody mentioned it to me earlier in the evening, and then Pinon Meade told me to look out for Harry. He said that Harry was in the White Horse, making war talk."

"I see," nodded Silent thoughtfully. "Is Pinon Meade a friend of yours?"

"Friend?" Sticky squinted narrowly. "No, I reckon not. You see, a fellow like me don't have friends, Slade. I've been branded a gunfighter, and people never figure that I'm like other folks, that I eat food like other folks, that I snore in my sleep and wear the seats out of my pants like other folks."

Silent did not laugh. He merely nodded. There

was nothing humorous in Sticky Clay's simile. It was rather pathetic.

"I reckon I know how you feel," said Silent. "I think—"

Just then Larry Neil ran into the saloon, yelling for the sheriff.

"Hey, Swan River! Clayton and old man Allenby just got here. They found Harry halfway between here and the Half-Circle Cross and brought him in. He's all shot to hell!"

The sheriff and Forty Dollar ran for the door-way, while there was a general exodus in that direction. Silent and Sticky joined the group.

People were gathering in front of the doctor's house because Larry Neil had spread the news aloud while looking for the sheriff. Swan River tried to keep everyone out of the house, but he allowed Silent to slip in.

Clayton and Allenby were at the bedside, watching Doc Edwell make his examination. Harry had been shot three times and was unconscious. One bullet had ripped through the fleshy part of his left shoulder, another moved lower through his left shoulder, and the third struck lower on the left side and seemed to have skidded off a rib.

"Shot from in front, eh?" observed Silent.

"Yes," nodded Allenby shakily. "Harry fired two shots at whoever dropped him. When he regains consciousness, we will know who shot him."

"And that killer is a good shot," said Silent softly. "He was shooting at the kid's heart. All three in the left side."

Allenby sat down beside the bed while Clayton left to get his supper. Silent watched Clayton leave; then he went outside and walked up to the Elk Saloon where he saw Clayton at the bar drinking.

At the bar was Frosty Welcome, the hotel proprietor, drinking with Joe Egan, his clerk. Frosty grinned at Silent and invited him to have a drink.

"I'm celebrating," Frosty explained a trifle thickly.

"Birthday?"

"No—not my birthday. I'm going out of the hotel business. Tired of it. And Joe's going to run the hotel. I'm going to be a cattleman again. Just bought me a ranch. Pay for it tonight."

"You going to have a big outfit?" asked Silent.

"Big enough. I'm going to blot all them 27A cows and register my old brand, the Circle W."

Silent nodded, declined another drink, and left the saloon. Irish was watching a card game, but he left and followed Silent. Silent led him to their horses and they rode out of town.

"Going to rain," said Irish. "Wished we had our slickers. I hate to get wet."

"Worse things than getting wet," grunted Silent.

Clouds blotted out the light from the sky, and they were forced to let the horses make their own way.

A dazzling flash of lightning, a crash of thunder, and the rain drifted at them in a solid wall of water, which quickly turned the deep dust into a muck of mud. They bowed their heads to the downpour and went on along the road.

Silent riding on the right side of the road, kept watching a fence until it came to a gate.

"C'mon, cowboy," he said. "Here's where we turn."

"Good," grunted Irish. "The water is running out of my boots right now."

Half a mile off the main road, as they were passing through a brushy spot, Silent swung his

horse into Irish's animal, forcing both mounts into
the brush and off the road. A few moments later,
a rider loomed up in the rain and went past them,
heading for Moolock.

It was impossible to know the identity of the
rider. They were about to move back into the road
when another rider, this one traveling at a gallop,
went past them, fairly splashing them with mud.
It was evident that this latter rider was anxious
to overtake the other.

"We can go on," said Silent. "It can't be much
further to the ranch. Maybe I've made a mistake,
but I don't think so."

About two hundred yards farther on, they came
to the blacker bulk of corrals and outbuildings.
From there they could see an open doorway, where
the light from an oil lamp illuminated part of a
buckboard and team that was standing close to
the porch.

They rode up and dismounted. No one was in
sight, but as they entered the kitchen, a voice called
out.

"What in hell is the matter now?"

Silent grinned at Irish, but did not reply. A moment later the speaker stepped into the kitchen,
a look of surprise on his face. He was a medium-
sized individual with a hooked nose and a scraggly
beard. His clothes consisted of a badly worn blue
suit, a moth-eaten fedora hat, and yellow boots.
Circling his waist, mostly hidden by his coat, was
a heavy cartridge belt, studded with ammunition.
Below the edge of the coat protruded the end of a
revolver holster. In his left hand he carried an old
yellow valise, bulging full.

"Huh!" he exclaimed explosively. "Where'd you
fellows come from?"

Silent did not reply. He squinted at the man and said:

"You're the cook, ain't you?"

"Yeah, I'm the cook."

"That's fine," grinned Silent, slapping his wet thighs. "We are hungry as hell, pardner."

"That's so, eh?" The cook leaned against the table. "Well, you're about half out of luck, gents. Right now I ain't got no time to do any cooking. I'm the only one at the ranch, and I'm going to town right away. Sorry, but it's got to be done."

"We'll pay you for the food," said Silent, ignoring the statement.

"Will, huh?" He shook his head. "Like I said, I'm going to town and I'm locking up the place."

"We'll cook our own meal and then lock up for you," said Silent.

"Not a chance. I don't even know you fellows."

"I'm Silent Slade."

The cook stiffened slightly at the sound of the name and his eyes shifted as he moistened his lips. Then he shook his head.

"Don't remember hearing it before," he said, trying to make his voice behave.

"No?" Silent grinned widely.

The cook shifted his feet as he placed the valise on the floor by the table, and his right elbow seemed to accidentally catch his coat and throw it away from the holster.

As he straightened up, his right hand flipped to his gun. It was a fast draw, which proved that the cook's experience with pots and pans had not caused him to forget how to draw a gun; but it availed him nothing.

His gun came to his waist level, but there was a nerveless finger on the trigger; nerveless be-

cause Silent's bullet had hit the cook dead center
before the latter's gun had hardly left its holster.
The cook's gun fell to the floor, while the cook slid
sideways, almost blocking the door from the
kitchen to the living area.

Irish coughed from the gunpowder fumes and
snapped his own gun back into the holster.

"Neat, and not gaudy," he commented dryly.
"He never knew what hit him, Silent. Why did he
go for his gun?"

"Scared," replied Silent. "My name got him."

Silent picked up the yellow valise and put it on
the kitchen table. Inside were a couple of shirts,
a miscellany of underwear, socks, red neckties,
and underneath all that were eighteen hundred
dollars in cash.

"Cooking pays well in this country," said Silent
when he finished counting the money. "Either that,
or he has saved about three years' salary intact."

Silent sat down at the table and carefully re-
placed everything in the valise. He looked around
the kitchen, his eyes searching. Suddenly he moved
forward in his chair, landed on his hands and knees
on the none-too-clean floor, looking at it closely.
Irish ducked sideways, the instinct of self-
preservation causing him to also land on his hands
and knees.

"What is it?" Irish demanded quickly.

"Get an ax!" exclaimed Silent. "Look outside—
at the wood pile!"

It did not take Irish long to acquire a desired
article. He soon handed the axe to Silent.

"What's the idea, Silent?"

"Take a look," said Silent. "They've got their
root cellar under the kitchen, and they've nailed
the door tight. Look at the fresh bruises on the

boards, cowboy. Look where they took the hinges off to make it look like it isn't a cellar. Get back."

At the risk of knocking down everything in the kitchen, Silent swung the heavy axe into the joint between the boards and tore the nails loose. Straight across one end of the former trapdoor he pried up the boards while Irish ripped them loose at the other end.

An odor of ancient vegetables and such drifted up to them, and a rickety stairway showed that Silent was right. Throwing the axe aside, Silent picked up a lamp and went down the stairs, with Irish close behind him, peering into the cellar.

Silent stumbled at the bottom of the steps, half turned and fell against the stairs. And as the lamp started to fall, Irish grabbed it and kept it from crashing. Silent managed to catch his balance and stand up. He had stumbled over the body of a man!

Silent looked down at the man, whose face was a mass of dirt and blood. Irish squinted beyond, where a girl crouched against the wall, her white face and staring eyes turned toward the lamp. It was June Allenby.

Silent knelt down by the body. It was Bud Bell. He peered up at Silent, his mouth wide open as he tried to spit out the dirt he had swallowed.

"Well," said Silent slowly, "we're all here, it seems."

"Slade?" Bud's voice was a whisper as he wiped his lips with the back of his hand. He shook his head and looked at June. "June, honey, we're all right. The—these men are friends."

The girl nodded slowly, helplessly.

"They had her down here quite a long time, don'tcha know?" said Bud slowly. "I—I went hunting for her, Slade. The last thing I remember was when I was eating in the 27A kitchen.

"There wasn't nobody but me and Lew Meeker, the cook, there. I heard a funny noise. It sounded like somebody calling. I asked Lew what it was, I think. Then something hit me, I reckon. Anyway, I woke up down here."

"Let's go upstairs," suggested Silent. "Can you walk, Miss Allenby?"

She nodded and made a brave attempt but failed. Silent caught her in his arms and carried her up to the kitchen, followed by Bud and Irish.

"They had me all tied up," she said wearily. "I got the gag loose and cried for help. In a few minutes they shoved Bud's body down the steps. I didn't know who it was, and he didn't move for a long time. When he came to, he had a few matches, and we found out who each other was."

"We heard the shot fired a while ago," said Bud as he looked at the body of the cook.

"How did you get the ropes off you?" Irish asked the girl.

"Bud did that," she said. "We heard them driving nails. It was like being nailed in a coffin. It was awful down there."

"You're a danged brave girl," said Silent. "You ran into a holdup, didn't you?"

She stared at Silent for several moments before she nodded.

"You knew the robbers, so they had to kidnap you, eh?"

She shut her lips tightly and shook her head.

"Then why did they kidnap you?"

"She won't talk about it," said Bud. "I've asked her a dozen times."

"That's all right," said Silent. "Bud, I want you to drive June back to town in the buckboard that's out in front while Irish and I go into town ahead of you."

Silent picked up the yellow valise and handed it to Bud.

"Take this with you," he said as he and Irish hurried out of the house.

As they mounted, they saw Bud helping June into the buckboard. He tossed the valise on the floor between them.

Silent and Irish spurred their mounts into a gallop and began throwing mud, while behind them came the 27A buckboard team, rain-soaked and eager to get warm.

It seemed that Moolock County was fairly well represented in town that night. Harry Allenby was still unconscious while his father sat at his bedside. Frosty Welcome had had too much to drink to consummate the purchase of the 27A, and he and Joe Egan were both propped up in chairs, passed out.

About ten o'clock, Joe Bass entered the Elk Saloon and found, to his chagrin, that one half of the deal was slumbering in a chair. Bass was mad. He shook Frosty viciously, and was rewarded with a loud snore from Frosty and a groan from Joe. The crowd objected to having Bass annoy Frosty.

Forty Dollar told Joe Bass to, "Get away from them, and let sleeping dogs lay."

Joe went away, swearing to himself, while Frosty cuddled down in his chair. Joe went across the street to the White Horse, where he found Lem Elder and Pinon Meade. Ed Clayton had just come from the doctor's house and reported no change in Harry's condition. He accepted a drink invitation from Joe Bass, who proceeded to tell him about Frosty Welcome.

"And he said he'd pay me cash for the ranch," said Joe cautiously. "He gave me five thousand the day before yesterday, and he said he'd give me the rest tonight at ten o'clock. He's too drunk now. Can't wake him up."

"How much is there left?" asked Lem anxiously.

"Still got an hour and forty minutes. But that ain't enough, I tell you. That fool can't sober up that quick."

"It's about time for Lew to show up, isn't it?" asked Pinon.

"To hell with him!" grunted Bass.

"What became of Slade and O'Day?" asked Elder. "They went away right after the doctor made his examination of Harry."

"Are you sure of that?" asked Clayton.

"Damn sure. I've been up and down both sides of the street. Their horses ain't at the racks and they ain't in none of the buildings."

Clayton and the three men from the 27A left the White Horse and went back across the street to the Elk. Frosty Welcome had slipped out of his chair and was now reclining on the floor. Joe Bass snorted an oath as they turned to the bar and ordered their drinks.

Sticky Clay came in and sat down near the door, watching the people. He looked more sinister than ever tonight. He knew that someone had suggested that he had met Harry Allenby and they finished their battle, but Sticky was not going to be frightened out of town by talk.

A few minutes later Old Hank came in. He looked around, saw Sticky, and sat down beside him. The four men at the bar noticed these two. Lem Elder drank only half of his liquor, wiped his lips with the back of his hand, and declared himself out of tobacco.

"Be back in a minute," he said and went out. At the doorway, he almost bumped into Frank Allenby, who was coming in. The three men at the bar turned to look at Allenby, and those at the games hesitated in their play long enough to listen.

"Harry is conscious," stated Allenby wearily. "But he refuses to tell us who shot him."

The crowd murmured their wonderment, and none of them saw Silent and Irish, muddy from their long trip, come in through the rear of the room. They came down behind a roulette layout, where half a dozen players were grouped, and stopped.

"Does he know who shot him?" asked Forty Dollar.

Swan River came in behind Allenby as Forty Dollar spoke.

"I'll bet he does," grunted the sheriff. "He's protecting somebody. If it was an even-break gunfight, he don't need to be scared to tell who got him."

"Are you sure he's conscious?" asked Pinon Meade.

"Yeah, he's conscious," nodded Swan River. "It's the queerest deal I've ever been up against."

"Most deals are queer," said Silent, coming toward the bar. His face was splashed with mud, and his clothes were sticky with the same substance. The crowd centered their attention on him now.

"Where you been, Silent?" asked Forty Dollar.

"Riding in the mud," grinned Silent. He turned to Joe Bass. "There's some low places on your road that you ought to bridge. A little rain makes a swamp out of them. My bronc turned over in one of them."

"In my road?" queried Joe Bass, squinting at Silent.

"Yes, out that way. I don't blame you for wanting to sell. If I had that kind of road—"

"Who wants to sell out?" asked Bass.

"You. Frosty told me he was buying you out tonight."

"Frosty?" Joe was both surprised and indignant.

"That's why he wanted to wake Frosty up," declared Forty Dollar. "I'll betcha forty dollars that's the reason."

Joe Bass shut his lips tightly. He did not want everyone to know that he was selling out. Clayton adjusted his necktie and started to walk away from the bar.

"Better stay where you are, Clayton," snapped a voice behind him, and he stopped, turned his head, and looked, but no one was there. "You ain't going no place, you know," added the voice.

Clayton backed against the bar, looking wildly about, wondering what was going on, while Silent, a smile on his lips, watched him closely.

"What—what's the meaning of this?" demanded Clayton.

"That was my friend out there," grinned Silent. "He and I were just thinking about something that happened two years ago."

"Two years ago?" questioned Clayton. "What do you know about anything that happened two years ago, Slade?"

Silent laughed and shifted his feet. "Some folks

might call it fortune telling, Clayton. I call it magic. Didn't you know that I could see into the past?"

"What kind of bunk is he talking anyway?" asked Joe Bass.

"Do you want me to demonstrate what I mean?"

"Hop to it," laughed Forty Dollar. "We'll all listen."

"All right. Now, I'm going into a trance. Watch me closely."

The games all ceased and everyone was interested. Silent's expression did not change, except that he looked more serious. Then he began.

"I can see two men riding through the hills. Down in a swale a man is squatting beside a little fire. He has two cows hog-tied near him. There's a running iron and an old fry-pan on the fire. He takes the hot fry-pan and vents the brands on the right shoulders of the animals. He comes back to the fire, takes the running-iron and draws a brand on each animal, just above where he has vented the original brands.

"Then I see the two men again. They see this man at the fire and he sees them. He jumps up, runs to his horse, and mounts. He has lost his hat but don't stop to get it. The men circle the hill, trying to head him off.

"These two men chase him through the hills, but he is too smart for them. The two men get separated. One of them circles back to the fire while the other keeps on after the rustler. The one that circled back dismounts at the fire. He looks at the animals, and then he looks all around. The fire is almost out.

"He puts the pan and iron into the fire again and puts on more fuel. Then he finds the rustler's hat. I can tell by his face that he knows who owns that hat. I can't see what he did with the hat, but it disappears from the picture.

"When the pan is hot again, he vents the brand that the rustler put on. It is a big vent now, almost covering the shoulder of both cows. Then he takes the running-iron and draws a brand on each cow's right hip. Now I can see him scatter the fire, look all around, and begin to look at the cows all over again.

"Then I see the other man ride back there, and they both talk. Now they ride away. I think they are talking about leaving the cows there for evidence."

Silent shook his head quickly and grinned.

"How do you all like that picture?"

Sticky and Old Hank had gotten to their feet, staring at Silent, wondering what he meant, where he had secured this information. Clayton's mouth was half open and he was breathing like a man suffering from a bad cold.

"What does he mean?" whispered Allenby. "I— I was one of those men—the one who kept on after the—"

"What kind of foolishness is this?" demanded Clayton. "I was the other man, and there wasn't anything like—"

Hank Bell was coming forward, staring at Clayton, who drew away from him.

"Hold everything, Hank!" snapped Silent. "I'd advise everybody to hold quiet. This is—"

Lem Elder came in through the open doorway and was halfway to the bar before he realized that the room was as quiet as a grave. He stopped suddenly, looking quickly around. His lips were twisted into a snarl and the skin seemed drawn tightly across his cheeks.

He looked at Silent, who was grinning at him, and his right hand opened and closed spasmodically.

"And that wasn't all the picture," said Silent slowly. "I might ask Lem Elder to stand perfectly still. You see it was like this. Allenby wanted to hire a detective. Clayton knew this, so he talked Allenby into letting him get one.

"Clayton wrote a letter to a man by the name of Jim Seeley. Seeley didn't last long. That was a mistake, I reckon. He wasn't supposed to be shot, but the party who shot him thought it was the right thing to do. I've got the letter that Clayton wrote to Seeley."

"What has the letter got to do with it?" asked Clayton. "I don't care who reads that letter."

"You should have asked Seeley to destroy it," replied Silent. "That letter plumb ruined things for you, Clayton."

"Ruined things?" Clayton's voice was hoarse.

"Yes, ruined things, Clayton," said a voice behind him as Silent again threw his voice. "Some folks don't read between the lines."

"Between the lines," muttered Clayton, looking over his shoulder, then back at Silent. "Magic! Bah!"

"Yes. Bud Bell went to the penitentiary, as innocent as I was of that charge," said Silent. "You knew it, Clayton! You were the man who came back to that fire and put on the HB brand. You knew who the rustler was. It gave you a hold over him and it put you in a position to steal Allenby's cattle.

"With the help of these men, you stole, shipped and sold all those Half-Circle Cross cows. The men who held up the train stole those two HB horses to make their getaway on, because the horses were so marked that there could be no mistake.

"You shared in that holdup. I don't know why Elkins, the stage driver, was killed, but he probably tried for his gun when June Allenby accidentally rode in on the holdup. I forgot to ask her about it."

"Ask her about it?" parroted Allenby wonderingly.

"She's over at the hotel by this time," said Silent. "I found her at—"

"Look out!" snapped Lem Elder. "By God, they're both over there, Joe! We're stuck!"

It took Lem's statement to electrify Clayton and the 27A outfit. Clayton threw himself away from the bar, drawing a gun from a shoulder holster, while Joe Bass, Pinon Meade, and Lem Elder shifted separately, each one streaking for his gun.

But they were caught between two fires. At the front door were Hank Bell and Sticky Clay, blocking their exit in that direction, while Silent and Irish prevented them from going out the rear.

Clayton was dead on his feet before his gun was out of the holster. From beside the roulette layout, Irish was shooting slow and carefully, while Silent flung himself against the end of the bar and shifted his gun from man to man, as he emptied it.

Joe Bass went down, and across him fell Lem Elder, flinging his arms wide, knocking Pinon Meade back against the bar, where he sagged for a moment before going down in a crumpled heap.

The room was filled with powder smoke until faces and forms were mere indistinct things. The crowd had had no chance for a getaway, but now they vaulted the bodies and ran outside, while those from the other saloons and business places met them with a volley of questions.

Sticky Clay had been hit twice, but not badly enough to make him want a doctor. Silent's right cheek was bleeding from a splinter which had been thrown at him from the bar, but Irish had escaped without a scratch.

The crowd, realizing that the fight was over, pushed back into the room, questioning, coughing, wondering what it was all about. Swan River and Forty Dollar did not stampede with the crowd, and it was Swan River who first examined the four victims. Joe Bass was the only one alive, still conscious, but fading fast.

"Shut up!" roared Swan River. "Joe's trying to whisper and I can't hear him."

Joe Bass was making a valiant effort to say something, but the words were slow in coming. The crowd grew silent as Joe's tongue began to function.

"Money...all...in...valise," he whispered. "Going...away...tonight...Sorry." He swallowed thickly. "Sorry...shot...Elkins. He... went...for...his...gun. Pinon killed...Seeley. I—I...guess that's...all."

"I guess that's enough," said Swan River, slowly getting to his feet. He turned to Silent. "I take my hat off to you and your magic, Slade. I don't know how in hell you did it, but you did."

"It wasn't too hard," said Silent wearily, looking at the empty gun in his right hand. "That letter was the key to it."

He drew out the letter after holstering his gun and spread it out on the bar top.

"Skip the first line and read every other line," he said.

Swan River leaned closer and read every other line. It read:

up against a very dangerous proposition and needs help...

you can make five thousand dollars for a few days' work....

and get away without the slightest chance of anyone...

knowing who you are, *sabe?*...

You will like Allenby. If you can't take this job, Jim...

it might make things very bad. Wire your decision.

"And that's what Clayton meant for Seeley to read, eh?" asked Forty Dollar, scratching his neck.

Silent nodded. "Yes, it seems that it was, Forty. If you notice, he had left plenty of room at the margins. I kind of kept looking at the letter, and I got to skipping around for the answer. I've heard of things like this being done before.

"I got to finding out a few things about Bud Bell's case, and I heard about the rustler venting the whole shoulder of them two cows. That wasn't according to Hoyle, and there must have been a reason. The big 27A outfit brand on the right shoulder.

"There was the rustler's hat, if you remember. If Clayton found that hat belonged to someone he wanted to protect or put the deadwood onto, what could be easier? But the first mistake was the burn out of the brand on the hip. The HB brands on the hip, and the HB was already in bad with the Half-Circle Cross. Does it look easier now?"

"It sounds good," grunted Swan River. "But that was kind of flimsy evidence, Slade."

"Worse evidence sent Bud Bell to prison. Somebody stole three hundred head of stock out of the loading pens the night we came to Moolock. The stock cars came too late to load that night, so they had to leave the cattle in the pens. Joe Bass got them cars, didn't he? I started guessing from there.

"They wasn't making enough money off Allenby's stock, so they started holding up trains and stages. They had to steal June Allenby to save themselves. Down in the dust of that road I found a red bead. It was just an ordinary bead—like them that ornament the pockets of Joe Bass's vest. It wasn't much, but it pointed the way.

"Me and Irish found June in the cellar of the 27A ranch tonight. Bud Bell went looking for her and got knocked on the head. They put him in a cellar with June, and nailed the door tight. I killed their cook. He knew that his cake was all dough, so he went for his gun. He had eighteen hundred dollars in his valise. I reckon that about closes the chapter."

"June is across the street?" asked Allenby. He had been in sort of a trance.

"Yes, she's over there," said Irish. "They didn't hurt her."

Allenby whirled and ran out. Bud came in. He knew now that he could look every man in the face. His convict brand had been wiped away.

"They told me about it, Slade," he said as he looked at the four men on the floor. "I don't know how it was done, but I'm glad. I'm not much on thanking anybody."

"You don't need to thank me, Bud," laughed

Silent. "Because you're welcome."

Over at the hotel, June Allenby was holding an impromptu reception, assisted by her father. As soon as Allenby saw Slade, he left the crowd and came straight to him.

"Slade, do you know what you've done? I've got my daughter back safe and sane—and everything is cleared up in the valley."

"Is the hate gone?" asked Silent.

"Hate?" Allenby shook his head. "Yes, I'm sure it's all gone."

June came up and took Silent's two hands and squeezed them.

"I don't know how I'm ever going to be able to thank you."

"That's all right," smiled Silent.

Allenby said, "Who was the man who was branding the cattle—the man whose crime was placed on Bud Bell?"

Silent squinted painfully for a moment. He looked at June, who was staring at him, her eyes pleading.

"That man." He hesitated. "That man was Pinon Meade."

"I see." Allenby nodded quickly. "I'm going over to ask Bud Bell and his father to forgive me, and then I'm going to write each of you a check."

Allenby fairly ran across toward the Elk Saloon and June moved in closer to Silent.

"Mr. Slade," she said softly, "I want to thank you for that. Joe Bass told me the whole thing. Blood is thicker than justice, at a time like this. Perhaps I was thinking more of my mother than of Pa."

"Maybe I was, too," smiled Silent.

"It's all right, now, you—you lovable liar."

Just then Bud Bell came running up to them and grabbed Silent by the arm.

"Slade, they're having a drink together—her father and mine! And her pa told me to come over and take care of her, while they talked about the future. Can you beat that?"

"No, you can't," smiled Silent, knowing that the hate in Moolock Valley was a thing of the past. "You take care of her, Bud. She's a game little girl and, by golly, she's worth taking care of. C'mon, Irish."

They walked away from the crowd and halted in front of the sheriff's office.

"Lovable liar," grunted Irish. "Huh! While you was in your trance, didja see who shot me and why?"

"One of them four on the floor," replied Silent. "Probably Clayton told them about us, so they thought they'd eliminate us."

"All right, that's good enough for me," sighed Irish. "I feel there must have been some sort of an agreement between Joe Bass and Harry Allenby before Harry tried to misbrand them two cows."

"I suppose there was," nodded Silent. "Allenby's stinginess drove the kid to steal. Clayton saved him from the pen, but his mistake was hiring Jim Seeley without telling Bass or Harry. Anyway, Clayton had some trouble with them—probably over their taking June—and they were thinking of eliminating him.

"Harry knew their game, but he drank and talked too much, so they tried to kill him. Very likely he knew where June was being held. There were just too many cooks—they spoiled the stew."

"Why did you pick on Pinon Meade?"

"It ain't my policy to shift guilt onto a dead man, but I reckon it won't hurt Pinon Meade's soul to have an extra cattle rustling charge on the books against him. June knows the truth and maybe she will be able to keep Harry going straight," said Silent.

Just then Swan River Smith came running down the walk, waving two checks in his right hand.

"Checks for you two from Allenby," he said, handing them the checks. "Them two jiggers, Allenby and old Hank Bell, sure do work fast. Allenby is buying the HB and making Bud foreman over all his belongings and hiring Sticky Clay to help out. Old Hank can stay on the HB as long as he lives. I never saw things change so damn fast."

"From hate to love," grunted Irish.

"Yessir," nodded Silent. "That's the way the world should be."